Conditions Apply

Derek Mortimer

Conditions Apply
and other stories

Conditions Apply and other stories
ISBN 978 1 76109 427 9
Copyright © text Derek Mortimer 2022
Cover image: Getty Images

First published 2022 by
Ginninderra Press
PO Box 3461 Port Adelaide 5015
www.ginninderrapress.com.au

Contents

Conditions Apply

Charles Robinson squinted through the window, trying to focus on the car pulled up outside the house. Ferocious sunlight bounced off the glossy duco. The car was an object of great beauty and power. With a car like that, you could go anywhere with anyone.

The driver got out, pushed his sunnies up the bridge of his nose to ward off the glare, flicked a speck of dust off the bonnet and checked his phone to make sure he had the right address. He tugged his shirt cuffs over big wrists then walked up the drive and rang the bell.

Charles opened the door and smiled up at the salesman.

'Good morning, sir, I'm looking for Mr Robinson. Is he home?'

'He is.' Charles extended his hand.

The salesman shook it, trying to hide his surprise. 'I'm Luke. Luke Little. Are you the Mr Robinson who wants a test drive of the Toyota Prada.'

'Speak up.'

'Are you the Mr Robinson who wants a test drive of the Toyota Prada?'

'I am.'

The salesman beamed back, trying to find a way of saying, how are you going to drive?

'I like the colour,' Charles said.

'Yes, white's very popular. But you can have any colour in the Toyota Prada – as long as it's white.' The salesman grinned. 'That's what the great American, Henry Ford, the founder of the car industry, boasted. Except that he said black. Any colour Ford as long as it was black,' the salesman smiled.

Charles nodded that he had heard and understood the joke. In fact, he had heard it many times. 'Can you push me to the car, Luke?'

Luke wedged the door open with his foot, took hold of the wheelchair handles and tentatively set off down the ramp into the heat.

'Not so fast! There's a curve halfway down,' Charles directed.

'I haven't driven one of these before.'

'That's evident.'

'Not my style. No, that's not what I meant, what I meant was…'

'I know what you meant.'

They reached the car and stopped.

'Is there anyone else?' the salesman asked.

'Just me. Are you going to help me in?'

'You want me to drive you, right? For the test run?'

'You're quick. My eyes are not very good these days.'

Luke helped Charles swing his backside then his legs into the car. There was a whiff of old man about him.

'I'm just about blind in one eye. Not good in the other. All that time I spent in the sun as a young man. I was a surfer. A good one. I'm going to be blind in both eyes according to the ophthalmologist, but the so-called experts don't know everything. I know more about me than they do.'

Luke carefully closed the door on Charles, ensuring nothing was trapped, and climbed in beside him.

'Come on, let's get going,' Charles ordered.

Luke loaded the wheelchair into the boot then got into the driver's seat. 'Anywhere in particular?'

'No. I just want to see how it runs. And things like what space I have. How big the boot is for the chair.'

They rolled smoothly down the drive, out of the sun-baked cul-de-sac and onto the main road.

'You by yourself at home?' Luke asked.

'I don't talk when I'm driving,' Charles told him.

'I wish more people were like that. There'd be far less accidents.'

'Fewer.'

'Fewer what?'

'Fewer, not less, accidents.'

Luke glanced at Charles out of the corner of his eyes.

'I want you to go through all these new gizmos with me – you know, satnav, cruise control, assisted parking, those things,' Charles said.

'Certainly.' Luke did.

Charles paid close attention but seemed to already know. Luke began to think that Charles had been through it all before. They ended the test run and halted outside the house. Luke lifted the wheelchair from the boot and helped Charles out of the car.

'Give me a push up the ramp, will you. I can do it myself but it's easier with help.'

Luke obliged, but the muscles in Charles's arms told him that the old man was used to wheeling himself around. He manoeuvred the chair up the ramp, through the door into the house and positioned it so Charles was looking out the window down at the car, glistening invitingly in the sun.

'What do you think?' he asked.

'I think it's a great car, just the thing.'

'Would you like me to organise registration, insurance and the rest?'

'Not yet.' Charles held up a hand. 'I need to think about a few issues first. I'll be in touch.' He shook Luke Little's hand.

'I…'

'Thank you for your time, Mr Little.' Charles reached out and pushed open the door. 'I'll be in touch.'

Luke Little walked down the ramp, slid into the driver's seat, sighed, shook his head and drove off.

*

Stephanie Robinson arrived in late afternoon. She swung her lycra legs off her bike, removed her helmet and fluffed out sweaty short brown hair. She tucked her helmet under her arm, pushed her bike up the drive and propped it against the roller doors of the garage, then she clack-clacked up the wheelchair ramp into the house. Her father was examining glossy brochures spread on the table.

'Superwoman,' he said without looking up.

'Hello to you too, Dad. What you up to?'

'I'm buying a new car.'

'You're what?'

'You heard me. Buying-a-new-car.'

'Dad, you're not allowed to drive.'

'I'll sort that out.'

'Ohh, you're not gonna start that again, are you?'

'I never stopped.'

'Be realistic. Face where you are in life. Make the best of the good things.'

'I am, I do. And I'm dealing with it. First, I'll get a new car, then the other thing.'

'The other thing is not gonna happen.'

'I'll make it happen, like I've made everything happen in life.'

'Dad! This is not like a business deal, it's not about persuading a client to accept what you're offering.'

'Don't tell me the obvious. I know how to sell something, particularly when that something's me.'

'Dad, I don't want to be brutal, but you, as a product, have very limited appeal. What woman wants a seventy-year-old lover…'

'Seventy's the new fifty.'

'…who's confined to a wheelchair, needs help to the toilet and shower, can hardly see, is hard of hearing and is incontinent?'

'It's only my bladder, not the other side, and it's only sometimes.'

'Dad, be satisfied with carers. Everybody else is.'

'Who said they're satisfied?'

'They accept where they're at in life. You need to do the same.'

'You trying to tell me I'm past it?'

'It, as you put it, is not the question.'

'Anyway, first I'll get the car, then I'll search. A good salesmen identifies the customer, then gets them to want what they're being offered.'

'Which is you?'

'That's right. Me.'

'No salesman's that good.'

'I'm offering what a woman wants: a home, financial security, comfort, affection. Whoever she turns out to be, that's what she'll get with me.'

'Then?'

'You're only worried you might have to share your inheritance.'

'Not true. I don't need it.'

'You need it all right. You're nearly forty, and you don't even have a mortgage.'

'Like thousands of others.'

'Nor a man.'

'Like thousands of others.'

'Men only last a couple of weeks with you. You're too independent. I told you, years ago, come into business with me, look after the office side, but no, you wanted to be a teacher. A teacher with a bicycle and a rented shoebox you call home. A teacher with pupils who are so stupid they don't know they're stupid.'

'It's not about me, it's about you. You'll get hurt…you'll make a fool of yourself.'

'You're jealous.'

'That's not the word I'd use Dad, but OK. Go ahead.'

*

Charles took her irony as support. He did what any red-blooded old man would do in this situation: he logged onto dating sites. And he lied a little.

There were lots of beautiful women out there. He was choosy, so it took a while for him to select the first one – Margaret, only twenty years his junior.

He booked a table at one of the best Italian restaurants on the north coast. He was wheeled in by a smiling taxi driver. Margaret, who by habit had arrived early, saw little resemblance in the man in front of her to the photo he had posted online. She left in a hurry, clutching her bag, before the waiter even had chance to spread a starched white serviette across her elegant cashmere thighs.

Charles persisted with the mature-age dating sites. The encounters all ended more or less the same, sometimes even quicker than with Margaret. Often, Charles was not the only one who had lied.

He was unperturbed. He tweaked his profile a little, provided a hint of his circumstances, a small hint, that a perceptive woman could pick up.

Eventually he found Jasmine.

Or did she find him?

*

Charles was pleased when she arrived at the Thai restaurant and didn't seem shocked to discover that her date was in a wheelchair. He had dressed up for the occasion. His usual baggy and comfortable shorts had been replaced with a pair of chinos matched with a pale blue long-sleeve cotton shirt. Instead of his usual velcro sandals, he wore light tan plaited leather Italian shoes. His hair was combed, his chin shaven smooth.

His date extended her hand. 'I'm Jasmine.'

Her handshake was firm for a woman, the skin on the palms of her hand surprisingly rough. She did not appear a delicate jasmine flower to Charles but she seemed OK; longish dark hair pulled in at the back, round suntanned face with broad features, solid build, a blue and green dress with short sleeves. Strong arms. He hadn't been able to check out her legs as she walked in. She sounded, and she looked, as far as he could see, which wasn't far, about half his age.

'Glad you could make it. Sit down.' Charles waved in the direction of the table. He was two-thirds the way through his ritual evening schooner of beer. He poured her a glass of white wine from a bottle waiting in an ice bucket. 'A good choice, Thai.'

She took a sip of her wine, set the glass down then placed her elbows firmly on the table and looked directly at Charles. 'Appearance and age don't matter to me. It's the heart of the person that counts,' she said.

'Good.'

They had both eaten the fishcakes and were waiting for the chicken skewers before she spoke again. 'I'm in the nursery business.'

'Kids! I admire you. How can you stand them at that age?'

'Plants. I grow plants.'

'Oh, right. Plants, you said?'

'Yes. I like trees best. Mountain ash is my favourite.'

'Can you speak up? My hearing's not the best these days.'

'My favourite tree is the mountain ash, Eucalyptus regnans. The best ones are in Tassie,' Jasmine said again in a voice so loud the manager hurried out from the kitchen to see what was wrong.

Charles handed him his smartphone and asked him to take a photo.

'They grow to one hundred and twenty metres high, the tallest flowering plants in the world,' Jasmine said, pausing long enough for the picture to be taken.

Charles nodded. 'Not the sort of plant for a window box then.'

'Not really. Do you like trees?'

'No. Nothing but leaves all over the place.'

Charles waited for a response, but Jasmine did not speak again until the chicken skewers were finished and she had licked the peanut sauce from her lips. She had a very healthy appetite.

'So, what do you want?' she asked.

'I've had enough, couldn't eat another thing.'

'No, in a relationship.'

'The usual.'

'Which is?'

Charles rested his hands on the side of his wheelchair. 'You know, companionship…that sorta thing. You're not married, are you?'

Jasmine laughed. 'No. Was once. It's a short story. Tell me more about yourself.'

'I want a woman's company. I see my daughter Stephanie most days. She's a teacher. I'm very fond of her, although she doesn't think so. But she's my daughter. My dear wife Elizabeth had a cerebral embolism and died five years ago.'

'Sorry to hear that.'

'One of those things. I'm gonna live forever, but I have to put up with these.' He rapped his knees with his knuckles, 'I was a champion surfer when I was younger. Elizabeth looked after the home and the kids and I built up a very successful manufacturing business so I could feed, clothe and house us and educate Stephanie. Work, family, surfing. A trifecta. You?'

'There's just me. Love my work. Hate my boss, Hunter. Jasmine's not my real name, but jasmine's my favourite plant, after the mountain ash, and if you're going to change your name, Jasmine's a better bet for a woman than mountain ash or Eucalyptus regnans, eh?' She grinned. 'And my name goes with my work, more or less. Grew up inner Sydney with Mum. That's about it.'

Charles waited for more, but it did not come. 'OK. And what do *you* want?'

'Companionship with someone who's dependable, who's not going to run off when my back's turned,' she replied.

That was more or less the end of the first date. Charles ordered two taxis. He took selfies of himself and Jasmine outside the restaurant. They shook hands and Jasmine kissed him on the cheek. Charles said he'd ring her.

*

Stephanie was waiting when he got home. 'What happened?' she asked as she pushed him up the ramp.

'It was our first date. Nothing! She's not that kind of girl.'

'Daaaad, stop it! What's she like? What did she say? What does she look like?'

Charles handed his smartphone to his daughter.

She flicked through the photos. 'She's ugly.'

'That's not a very…what is it?…feminist thing to say.'

'I'm not a feminist, I'm a daughter.' Stephanie held the selfies close to her father's face, 'Look. No wonder she didn't do a runner when she saw you.'

14

'She looks all right to me.'

'That's the last you're going to see of her. An expensive restaurant, a good feed and a bottle of good wine, paid for by a delusional old man. It's probably her regular monthly treat, preying on old men.' Stephanie dropped the phone on the table. 'Dad, let's stick to carers, OK? Gloria'll be in as usual tomorrow to get you up, showered, dressed and moving.'

'She won't.'

'Won't what?'

'Be here. She didn't turn up today. She was just like the rest, no sense of fun.'

'Again? All your carers had no sense of fun? Leyla? Marie? Mary? Olivia? Isabella? Is that's what's wrong with them?'

'Don't go on about it. They'll send someone else.'

'Then the same thing?'

'It's pretty late. Are you staying the night? The bed's made up in the guest room.'

'I'll go home.'

'Have you got someone waiting?'

Stephanie sighed, 'Do you want a hand into bed?'

'I can manage.'

'Good night.' Stephanie kissed him on the top of his bald head. 'And think about what I said.'

*

Charles pulled himself upright on the trapeze above his head. He manoeuvred his legs over the side of the bed and struggled into his clothes, then on to his wheelchair, muttering unkind words about carers. He wheeled himself into the kitchen where he made a sparse breakfast of toast, marmalade, tea. It didn't match Elizabeth's. Forty-three years of orange juice, boiled or scrambled egg and toast. He did a mental calculation: 15,695 breakfasts, give a week or two. Home helps did not get eggs of any kind right. They seemed to think he wanted soft spoiled eggs, not soft boiled eggs. Charles sat chomping on his toast in his favourite place, a small table near the window, overlooking the drive and the dozen or so houses with their neatly mown green lawns arranged along each side of the cul-de-sac. A radio hung from a hook on the window frame. It was tuned in to his favourite talkback station. Behind him was the kitchen-dining area. Elizabeth had persuaded him after a long time to have the room modernised and an island bench installed. She had died the week after it was completed. Charles only used it when there were other people. It felt like he was sitting on a bar stool in a pub.

A car drew up outside the house. A man got out. He walked up the ramp and pressed the bell.

Charles wedged his toast in his mouth and rolled to the door, 'Yesss?' he said through the toast and the fly screen.

The man was very large and dark-skinned. He was wearing a short-sleeve white shirt with a logo on it and neat shorts over thighs that were like knotted steel cables. The man also had blue lines across his face as though he'd gone head first through a car windscreen and the scars hadn't healed properly.

'G'morning. Charles? I'm Tawhiri. I'm your new carer from Cared-for.'

Charles removed the toast from his mouth. 'A man!'

'Last time I checked, yeah.'

'I usually have a girl.'

'I know.'

'I didn't realise Cared-for employed men.'

'Some of our clients don't mind.'

'Why men? Girls are more gentle.'

Tawhiri stood, blocking out the sun. Charles slowly opened the screen door and Tawhiri stepped in. Charles realised that what he thought were scars on the man's face were tattoos.

'OK. Looks like your breakfast's taken care of. Good man. How about the rest?'

'I'm not going to be showered by a man,' Charles said.

'I won't peep.'

'Beg your pardon?'

'Accepted. How about I check what's in the fridge then, see if you need any shopping. Bed making? Fill your pill box?'

'My daughter shops. I can fill my own pill box. I just need help showering, so I don't drown, or get dumped again. And the house cleaning. And the bed making. Things that women do best. Showering can wait.'

'I see.'

'Will Gloria be here tomorrow?'

'Nah.'

'The day after?'

'Nah.'

'Some other girl?'

'Nah.'

'The day after that?'

'Nah.'

'Why?'

'Charles, you're a man of the world, you understand.'

'I'm going to complain to the agency. I'm not having this.'

'We'll get along great, man.'

'We won't. This is just for today. The cleaning stuff's in the cupboard next to the bathroom.'

Charles watched as Tawhiri scooped up the buckets and sprays and mops and brushes with his big hands. 'I suppose your name has a meaning,' he said.

'Storm. Tempest,' Tawhiri said, standing tall.

'Sounds like a toilet disinfectant. What's a man doing cleaning houses and showering senior citizens who are near their use-by date?'

'I've got six brothers in Auckland. I'm the eldest. The youngest's fourteen. They all think I do security at a nightclub. Big man job, eh. I did one month at the Fat Pussycat on the Gold Coast.' He shook his head. 'The men drank beer. Then they started fighting. Bad news. I don't like people hurting people – or people hurting me. I share a house with three useless Kiwis who can't cook. They buy takeaways. I cook proper food. I'd rather be deported than buy takeaway,' Tawhiri said. 'Roast chicken is my specialty.'

Roast chicken was the only thing he could cook, but Charles wasn't to know that.

'What about that stuff on your face? Does that mean something as well?'

'It's a moko, a traditional Maori tattoo.'

'Is it there to scare the hell out of people?'

'No. It shows tribal links.'

'Tribes? You still have tribes?' Charles took a deep breath. 'Well, a bit different to the faces I'm used to. I…'

Tawhiri looked at his watch. 'I'll get started.'

*

Charles took Jasmine out to dinner again. He told her some of his past life, the surfing he had loved but now hated and wouldn't go near the ocean, but wouldn't say why. Jasmine told him about plants and trees. Charles hadn't given much thought to plants and trees before; they were just there. He learned a lot from Jasmine, an interesting woman. Like Stephanie said, she wasn't exactly beautiful, but until he was really close Charles couldn't tell. And he wasn't really close. Yet.

After Charles had taken Jasmine out to dinner three or four times, Stephanie phoned her father and said, 'I want to meet this woman.'

'Your shoebox or my home?' her father said.

'Yours. But I'm not cooking.'

'You don't know how too. We'll get takeaway.'

Jasmine arrived wearing a blue and green dress. It wasn't the same as the one she wore on their first date but Charles couldn't see the difference. She drove up in an old ute which had a large pot plant tied in the back.

'It's a lilly-pilly, Syzygium smithii. You can grow it on your balcony,'

Jasmine said to Charles, who was sitting in his wheelchair at the top of the drive waiting, the evening sun warm on his legs.

'I don't have a balcony.'

As Jasmine wrestled the plant out of the ute, Stephanie called out in a voice that belied her sarcasm, 'Do you want Dad to give you a hand with that?'

Jasmine ignored her and lifted the lilly-pilly to the ground, trying to keep it clear of her dress. 'It'll not grow as big as a mountain ash.'

'I won't have them greenies protesting outside if I decide to cut it down in a few years and sell the timber then?'

'Guaranteed not.'

As well as the tree, Jasmine had a dozen cans of beer for Charles, a bottle of red wine, and a bunch of peace lilies. The pizzas arrived a short time later, one Loaded Supreme, one Chicken and Camembert and one Traditional.

Stephanie spread the pizzas out on the dining bench.

'Not in the boxes,' Charles said in exasperation.

'It'll save washing up.' Stephanie pulled a wedge off, put it onto his plate then did the same for herself. After second thoughts, she asked Jasmine, 'Which one?'

'Whatever. Thanks.' Jasmine poured the wine and the beer, the three said 'Cheers' in unison then started to eat in silence.

'Jasmine likes to eat well,' Charles said.

'I can see that,' Stephanie replied.

'It's hard work running a nursery,' Charles added. 'Takes a good business head.'

'So, what are we going to talk about, relationships, trees, plants, cars, getting old?' Jasmine asked.

'I know what we're not going to talk about: knee operations, back operations, who's got dementia, who spends their days in hospital sitting by the bed of a comatose partner, who's died,' said Charles. 'That's all old people talk about.'

'What do you want from my father?' Stephanie asked Jasmine, with a forced smile.

'They even discuss their favourite films but they can't remember the titles, the names of the actors, nor what they were about,' Charles said, trying to keep the uninvited guest out of the room.

Jasmine chewed on her pizza for a moment before answering. 'The usual: money, a big house, a business, you know, stuff.' She waited for a few beats in the silence before adding, 'I don't want any of that, if it's what you think.'

'What do you want from him then?'

'The same as he wants from me.'

'Reeeeally?' said Stephanie in mock surprise.

'Why not?' Jasmine said.

'Do you want me to go into detail?'

'If that's what floats your boat,' Jasmine told her.

'Here's to the future!' Charles raised his glass and looked hopefully at each of the women. His attempt to re-route the conversation failed.

'People go on dating sites because they want to love and be loved. Is that why you chose Dad? He's twice your age and not exactly an area of outstanding natural beauty.'

'I'll be around longer than you. Parents often bury their children these days,' Charles replied testily.

'Dad, I'm just facing facts and consequences. You don't have all that many years left. Is that the appeal for you, Jasmine?'

Jasmine suppressed a smile. 'Why did you go to a dating site?' she asked Charles in a soft voice. 'Why did you choose me?'

'Because everyone else fled when they saw him,' Stephanie replied. She thought, men probably ran from you too, but didn't say so.

'I've made my choice, Jasmine's made hers. We're going to get on with it and see what happens,' Charles said.

'And you expect me to sit and watch?'

'No, turn your back. But you could miss something interesting, educational even,' said Charles.

'Something bloody hysterical more likely, Dad.'

'Entertaining for everyone then,' Jasmine added. 'What are you worried about, Stephanie?'

'Her inheritance,' Charles said.

'Oh Dad, it's not that.'

'I don't need anybody's money,' Jasmine said dismissively. 'I have my job at the nursery.'

'I thought you owned the nursery,' Stephanie exclaimed.

'I didn't say that.'

'A woman on her own has to work, not like when she's married and being provided for,' said Charles.

'You wouldn't let Mum work, or have any independence.'

'Charles knows what he wants and what I want, that's all that matters. We'll leave it at that, eh?' Jasmine stood up abruptly. 'See you tomorrow.' She leaned over, rested both hands on Charles's shoulders, kissed him on the cheek and headed for the door.

'Aren't you going to toilet and shower him, then put him to bed before you go?' Stephanie shouted after her.

*

A routine developed. A courtship, you might say. Charles and Jasmine would eat out three or four times a week; a couple of times a week they would share Charles's ritual late afternoon drinks at the window overlooking the green lawns and lonely hibiscus bushes of the street and the solitary lilly-pilly standing sentinel beside the garage. Then they would have a takeaway delivered. Stephanie was there those times, not because she was invited but because she was still trying to work out what Jasmine was after.

The shared dinners for three were not the most comfortable meals of the week for anyone except Charles. He enjoyed the extra attention and ignored the conflict.

Friday night was Jasmine's night at home. Nothing was allowed to interfere with that. She was totally inflexible on the issue. So Stephanie and Charles ate together as they used to.

*

One day, Charles asked Jasmine to got to the house a little earlier. She arrived in her ute and parked in the drive. Charles was waiting outside. He pushed the remote control and the garage shutter doors rolled slowly and smoothly upwards. Inside was a glistening white, new Toyota Prada.

'Wow! You've been treating yourself,' Jasmine said.

'No, I've been treating you. Conditions apply.'

'Me! And what conditions?'

Charles laughed. 'We'll talk about that later. But what do you think to the Prada?'

'I've got my ute.'

Charles snorted. 'I'm not driving around in that old thing with trees growing in the back, dead leaves in the glovebox and caterpillars crawling all over me. You will drive me in the Prada whenever we're out. The rest of the time you have it if you want. But no plants in the boot. It's a car not a tree farm.'

Jasmine was overwhelmed with Charles's generosity.

So was Stephanie. 'You've what?' she yelled in horror. 'It's bribery.'

'The whole of life's bribery, Steph. This is payment for services rendered.'

'Services! I take it you've told her what services you expect. You're a cynical old man.'

'Why the fuss? I wanted to get a car for you years ago but you said no.'

'Exactly. You were trying to bribe me. Did you pay cash?'

'It's on a tax business deal. The accountant organised everything.'

'When will she have time to drive you anywhere? She works in the nursery all day.'

'I'll sort that out. It's my car in my name, she just feels that it's hers. It's marketing.'

'Oh, not that again. It is her car, except you've paid. What else are you going to give her?'

'Who knows.'

*

Jasmine dropped off another plant for Charles on on her way to work – Hibiscus syriacus. She didn't particularly appreciate tropical hibiscus plants but thought that Charles would. He liked things that were controllable. She arrived at the same time as Tawhiri for his shift.

'He's only here until they send another girl. His name's Tawhiri,' Charles explained to Jasmine as she walked into the house.

'Pittosporum tenuifolium,' Jasmine said.

'What are you talking about?' Charles asked testily.

'Tawhiri's the name of a small New Zealand tree. Family, pittosporaceae. Genus, pittosporum,' Jasmine said.

'He,' Charles jabbed his finger in the direction of Tawhiri, 'told me it meant tempest.'

'A tempest or a tree, whichever you want.' Tawhiri laughed.

'True,' Jasmine said. 'It's also called black matipo.'

'That would be right. Black whatever, tempest, tree, toilet disinfectant, it's all the same to me because he'll be gone in two shakes of a lamb's tail.'

'What happened to the last carer?' Jasmine asked.

'She moved,' Tawhiri said, trying not to smile.

'Really?' Jasmine said.

'She had no sense of fun. I've complained about the replacement,' Charles said, nodding in the direction of Tawhiri.

'What's wrong with him?' Jasmine asked.

'What's wrong? Look at his face. It frightens the hell out of me. I used to have Gloria smiling at me every morning. Now I have Tawhiri doing a haka on the front lawn. At least it keeps my bowels open.'

'Charles!' Jasmine suppressed a laugh.

'You couldn't bring kids round here with him in the house.'

'I didn't know you had grandchildren,' Jasmine said.

'I don't, as far as I know anyway, but if I did I wouldn't bring them here. I had a nightmare the day he arrived. It started off with him pushing me into the shower and ended with me being boiled in a big iron pot on a fire.'

'Stop it, Charles,' Jasmine said.

Tawhiri laughed at him. 'Charles an' me are good mates really.'

Charles grunted.

'You ready for your shower now, Charles?' Tawhiri asked, still laughing.

Charles took a deep breath, spun his wheelchair round and headed for the bathroom.

*

Charles took Jasmine to the theatre, Henrik Ibsen's *A Dolls House*. He had once taken Elizabeth to see the musical *Oklahoma*, her sixtieth birthday. She enjoyed it. So did Charles. They vowed they would see more shows but Charles was a busy man and they had not got round to it.

Jasmine had never been to a live performance, except music gigs in Ballina pubs. Charles didn't read anything about *A Dolls House*, other than the title. He thought it was about dolls – not kid's dolls, but dolly women – and would be a bit of fun.

Jasmine went to Charles's house straight from work. He showed her into the guest room so she could change. A large white bed draped with a mosquito net was set against the wall. Drawers, each with a reading lamp, sat on both sides of the bed. A dressing table stood against another wall. Jasmine spread a bright green dress on the bed, cursing her rough hands that caught on the silk. She showered and dressed. Charles smiled when she walked into the lounge room swinging her hips.

Jasmine loved the little theatre, and the play. 'Wow,' she said as she was driving Charles back home, 'that woman, Nora, was amazing. She really went for what she wanted. Nothing got in her way, even kids.'

'If she'd had a car, she would have driven over them in her rush to get out. A dreadful woman. She had everything, good husband, good home, three good kids, all the things a woman could want. And she abandoned the lot. What about the husband? What about the kids? A selfish woman. Utterly.'

'I think he did all right out of it. He got the kids, the home,' Jasmine told him.

They glided up the drive to Charles's place in the shiny white Prada. Jasmine got out, lifted the wheelchair from the boot and helped Charles into it. She pushed him up the ramp, through the door. 'There you go. Thanks for a lovely time. It was really great. Made you think about things, didn't it?'

'Like what?'

Jasmine didn't try to answer. She placed her hands on the wheelchair, leaned over and kissed Charles on his lips. He was about to speak, but was stopped by the kiss before the words reached his tongue.

'Do you need help?' Jasmine asked, cocking her head to the side.

Charles took her hand. 'I'll be all right. Tawhiri will do the showering in the morning.'

'He's OK then? Is he as good as a woman?'

'Not possible.'

'That's nice to know.'

'Why don't you stay the night, save driving home? There's the guest room,' Charles said tentatively.

'I can't.'

'Why? Who's waiting at home?' Charles asked suspiciously.

Jasmine hesitated. She thought about it a little longer. 'OK then. Just tonight.'

Charles released her hand. 'Done!' He smiled. 'Come on.' He rolled along the hallway and Jasmine followed.

Charles pushed aside the door to the guest room and Jasmine stepped in. 'If there's anything else you want, you know where I am.' He paused for a moment and smiled, hopefully.

'I'm fine.' It was Jasmine's turn to smile. 'Are you sure you'll be all right?'

'Of course.' Charles slowly reversed his wheelchair and rolled back down the hall to his bedroom. He sighed resignedly.

Jasmine looked at herself in the mirror above the dressing table. She carefully took off the green dress and hung it on a coat hanger in the empty wardrobe. She picked up her mobile and pecked out a number.

Tawhiri arrived next morning as Jasmine was leaving.

She rolled the window of the ute down as they drew level with each other. 'Mr Black Matipo.'

'G'day, sweet-smelling flower,' he said, with a hint of sarcasm. 'What a surprise to see you here. Or not.'

'An easy shift for you today. Showering done. Breakfast done.'

'I'll soon be out of a job!' Tawhiri called as she drove off into the glare of the morning sun.

*

A regular pattern developed. On the nights they dined out, Jasmine went to Charles's house after work. She showered, changed into a dress, sat with Charles for an evening drink then drove them to a restaurant. When they came home, she helped Charles get undressed and into bed then went home. Most nights.

During the day, after Tawhiri had been and gone and Jasmine was at the nursery, Charles wheeled himself into her room. He would take her dress from its hanger, lay it across his lap and place the palms of his hands on the soft fabric. He would lift the dress to his face and inhale; musky perfume, the smell of a woman.

His home had once been full of women things: Elizabeth's dresses, and hats and shoes, perfume and talc, the smell of dinner cooking while he and Elizabeth sat looking out of the window as the the sky paled and the heat went out of the day. He would drink a cold beer while Elizabeth sipped a G and T. Life was work, work, work. He loved it, and what he was building. He brought in the money, Elizabeth ran the home and looked after Stephanie. He was king in his castle.

*

Over a few weeks, more clothes appeared in the guest room wardrobe:

dresses, jeans, T-shirts, shorts, shoes. The drawers by the side of the bed which previously held nothing but air, now contained underclothes; bras, and things silk, soft as hibiscus petals, some elaborately trimmed with black lace. Charles nodded. He obviously knew they were knickers, but he didn't know they were called French knickers.

Jasmine noticed that the clothes had been moved. She smiled with satisfaction.

*

One weekend, Jasmine drove Charles to Ballina markets. She bought him a leather belt. He bought her a new pair of work boots. Later, they drove the narrow back roads of the lush green hinterland.

Charles would not allow Jasmine to stop off for coffee at any of the villages. 'They used to be real places where country people lived and bought their stuff,' he complained. 'Now they're full of Ye Olde Tea Shoppe tourist places that sell smelly candles, weird little figures made out of banksia tree seeds and old fence posts and incense dream-catchers, lemon myrtle tea, and everybody walks up and down the street saying, "Love you. Love you."' He turned and looked up at Jasmine, 'But thanks for bringing me out. It was nice. I enjoyed the fresh air. Maybe we can go for coffee to your place on the way back.'

Jasmine emphatically rejected the suggestion. 'It's just a pokey little rented house, your place is much more comfortable,' she told him when he persisted.

'I'll bet you're hiding someone.'

'Yeah! A secret lover?' she produced a mocking lascivious leer.

'Could be.'

Jasmine smiled. 'What would I want with a secret lover?'

'Same as anyone else.'

'How about we drive up to Surfers Paradise next weekend? We can walk along the promenade and have a coffee in one of the new places.' Jasmine stressed the word new, knowing there were no Ye Olde anythings in Surfers.

Charles shook his head vigorously. 'No.'

Jasmine pulled the car over at a vantage point in the hills. She helped Charles into his wheelchair and they went for a walk. She rhapsodised over the view of forested ridges and valleys that ran in folds east to the distant sparkling ocean.

'If we went to Surfers, you could help me improve my swimming. I can never catch a wave,' Jasmine said.

'I've just told you, no.'

'Why? You'd make a good teacher.'

'It's not a question of teaching.'

'What then? You used to love swimming. You told me, a champion surfer.'

'I hate swimming.'

'That's un-Australian,' Jasmine said in mock horror.

'You going to dob me in?'

'Definitely.'

Jasmine dropped the subject and turned her attention instead to trees, the eucalypts that grew tall and straight, leathery leaves hanging still in the heat. She sang out names: yellow box, wattle-leaved peppermint, red-barked sassafras, grey gum, forest red gum, blackbutt. When she stopped, there was only the sound of wheels on gravel, and the distant rumble of thunder.

They turned round when the first warm drops of rain exploded in the dust. By the time Jasmine had Charles in the car, the chair in the boot, and herself in the driver's seat, water was was streaming down her face and her soaked T-shirt and jeans clung to her. As she moved to turn on the ignition, Charles stayed her hand.

'I'll tell you why.'

Jasmine had to strain to hear what Charles was saying as the rain roared on the roof and cascaded down the windscreen.

'The beach has bad memories. Like I said that first night at dinner. I was a surfer, a good one. Really good. A young man who could dance on water. I thought I'd do it forever.' Charles stopped.

Jasmine took his hand. Despite the heat and humidity, it was cold. 'Then?'

'And I did keep on. Then, six years ago I was dumped by a massive wave and landed on my head. Overnight, I became useless. Not much good for anything. Elizabeth had to look after me. It was a big strain on her. She collapsed and died a year later.'

Charles sat, breathing slowly in and out. 'Just the sound of the ocean brings it all back. The roar of water as it crashed on top of me. Tumbling around in the surf, bursting to come up for air. It had all happened before of course, but that day… Then, lying on the beach, someone saying, "Don't move him." Eventually being stretchered off, helicoptered to hospital, my mate saying, "You'll be all right, Charles," as they loaded me aboard. If only I had stayed away that day. If only I'd looked at the waves and said no, too bloody rough today, go home.'

'If only.'

'If only.'

'Life has if only moments for us all. No good blaming yourself,' Jasmine said.

They sat and she waited for Charles to say more, but there was nothing more to be said.

The roar of the rain on the roof eased to a patter, then stopped. Jasmine started the engine and turned on the wipers.

Charles did not speak again until they were home and Jasmine had changed out of her wet clothes. She made coffee and they sat at the window.

When Charles had drained the last drop of coffee from his mug, he said, 'I've told you about me. Now it's your turn. Tell me more about you. All I really know is that you grew up in Sydney with your mum, and you're a tree-hugger.'

'There's not much else to tell.'

'Tell anyway.' Charles wheeled himself into his bedroom and Jasmine followed.

She helped him onto the bed.

He stretched out, sighed. 'Being driven around is tiring,' he joked. He patted the bed by his side. 'Jump up here where I can hear you better.'

Jasmine climbed onto the bed. She settled in, stretched her large brown hands on her thighs, and was silent for a moment. 'Right, Dad died when I was nine. Mum was more interested in having fun than in having me around. She had a series of live-in boyfriends and passing-through boyfriends.'

'Sounds an awful way to bring up a kid. Worse than that Nora woman in the play. Did they, you know, hurt you?'

Jasmine sighed. 'Nah. They were just a bloody nuisance. Mum loved me but she loved herself more.'

'The government should have tests to determine whether people are fit to become parents.'

Jasmine shook her head. 'Nobody knows whether you're gonna be a good mother or not, until it happens.'

Charles took her hand. 'Or a good father.'

'I left school at fifteen, worked as a checkout chick and other shit jobs. That first year, I saved enough money to go to Tassie on holiday with a girlfriend. It was, Wow! I saw my first mountain ash. It was in the Styx forest. They're the biggest, the most beautiful tree in the world. It takes half a day to walk around the base of some of them.'

'What?'

'OK, I lie sometimes, but you know what I mean. Even you'd be impressed.'

'I knew you were a greenie. You weren't in the anti-logging protests, were you?'

'No, but I shoulda been. Back in Sydney, I found a job at a community nursery providing trees for residents and the council. They weren't mountain ash that we grew, but they were trees. The rest, like they say, is history. I'd found home. Enough info? I'm tired. Bedtime.' Jasmine leaned over and kissed Charles on the cheek.

'Stay.' Charles took hold of her shoulder. 'Tell me some more.'

Jasmine paused a moment. 'OK.'

Charles let go of her shoulder and took her hand.

'I went to TAFE at night and studied botany and silviculture. I lost my job during council cutbacks. Eventually, I found this nursery near Ballina where I'm overworked and underpaid and I'm bullied by my boss Hunter. I'm getting out ASAP.'

'I can't imagine you being bullied, Jasmine.'

'Well, when jobs are hard to get… Anyway, that's it,' she said with finality.

'What about the husband you mentioned?'

'It didn't last long.'

'Sorry to hear that.'

'I wasn't much more than a kid. He went out one night and didn't come back. That's the past. You've gotta think only of the future.' Jasmine sat up. 'I'm going. Got a big day ahead.'

Charles kept hold of her hand. 'Stay here with me.'

Jasmine shook her head.

'Why not?'

'Not tonight.'

'Come on.'

She shook her head again. 'Nah.'

'How about if I say please?'

'Say it.'

'Please.'

'Still no.' Jasmine laughed playfully.

'What's it going to take?'

Jasmine disentangled her hand.

'OK then. I'll see you in the morning.' Charles sighed.

Jasmine swung her legs off the bed and walked to the door. There was no need to rush with Charles.

'Good night,' Charles called after her. 'I did say, conditions apply.'

She smiled as she undressed and climbed in to her bed.

*

Stephanie leaned her bike against the garage wall, took off her helmet and teased out her sweaty hair. She hooked the helmet over the saddle and walked up the ramp. It was Friday, a Jasmine-free night. She was home, doing whatever she had to do on a Friday night.

On the way to the shower, Stephanie checked out the guest room. She slid open the wardrobe and flicked through the hanging clothes. She opened the bedside drawers and saw the French knickers. Why such an exotic choice? For whom such an exotic choice? Women didn't wear French knickers to keep their bums warm.

'Just in time,' Charles said when Stephanie came back. He had taken a bottle of wine from the fridge and placed it next to his beer on the little table by the window. 'You don't get breath-tested on a bike if I remember rightly.'

Stephanie ignored the oft-repeated remark. She wondered if he'd been shown the knickers yet. On? Or off?

'How's it going, Dad?'

'It?' he smiled.

Stephanie sighed. 'You know what I mean. How is the relationship progressing, if you want me to be formal about it?'

'Well.'

'Which means?'

'Very well.'

'Has she proposed yet?'

'No. She's trying not to rush things. Must take a lot of willpower.'

'I hope to God you haven't and she doesn't.'

'Still worried about your inheritance, Stephanie? You'll be taken care of.'

'I wasn't. I'm not. And I won't be.'

'Good.'

Stephanie had to admit to herself that Charles was more sprightly than she had seen him in years. Something was good in his life.

'You're putting on weight, Dad. All that wining and dining. It's bad for you. The heart. Diabetes.'

'I agree, it can lead to all sorts of things.' Charles smiled.

'So, a salad dinner?'

'Don't get carried away. There's plenty of real food in the fridge. I'll talk to you while you cook.' He poured her a glass of wine. 'That'll help keep you going. You can tell me what you've been up to.'

*

Stephanie increasingly called by the house on her way to school, just to check. Tawhiri became the sounding board for her worries.

'What do you think of Jasmine?'

'She's a cheerful woman,' Tawhiri replied.

'Yeah. That's obvious.' Stephanie hesitated. 'What do you think she wants?'

'You mean, young woman, old man. A father? Maybe something else. I'm just a carer, I wouldn't know.'

'Yeah, sorry, I shouldn't have asked.'

'No worries.'

It was all right for Tawhiri to say 'wouldn't know'. It wasn't his seventy-year-old father in a weird relationship. Jasmine didn't just want to dine out a few nights a week at Charles's expense, that was for sure; he wasn't exactly brilliant company. When her mother was alive, they'd sit night after silent night watching TV.

But he was happy, wasn't that the main thing? He had a companion. What other man in his condition could claim that? Old men in wheelchairs paid for full-time professional carers, twenty-four/seven. He paid in a different way for a more personal attention. It didn't matter what anyone thought. Tawhiri took care of him in the day, Jasmine took care of him in the evening, she, Stephanie, was there if needed. Stephanie felt that maybe she should be more concerned about what her father expected.

*

Tawhiri sometimes arrived when Charles was already at his small table by the window eating a breakfast made by Jasmine, dipping toast into a soft-boiled egg and drinking tea.

'G'morning, Charles. What needs doing?'

'Not much. I've had my shower. Smell me, I'm clean as a baby's bum.'

'Thanks for the offer, Charles, but I'll pass. And don't you mean soft as a baby's bum?'

'No.'

'OK. So, what do you want?'

'Just the cleaning.'

'No hurry then.'

'You can make me more toast. And some for yourself.'

Tawhiri took the fresh toast back to Charles and they munched and sipped their teas.

'You've got a girl as well as me looking after you, eh,' Tawhiri said.

'No.'

'She looks like a girl to me.'

'Oh she's a girl all right. But she's part of the household, my companion, not someone sent by the agency to look after me. She's not a carer but she takes care, and she doesn't complain to the boss, like some.'

'Yah got what you wanted then, Charles.'

'Soft-boiled eggs and toast?'

Tawhiri laughed and brought his hand down on his thigh with a smack. 'Charles, how?'

'How what? How do I get soft-boiled eggs?'

'You know, how'd yah get a girlfriend, at your age? I don't have a girlfriend. I live in a share house with three hairy-arsed kiwis on temporary work visas.'

'I'm not interested in the anatomy of your friends. I hope you're not either.'

'Come on, Charles, tell me.'

'You're my homecare not my confessor.'

'What's the secret?'

'You're stepping over the line.'

'It's not because you're handsome.'

'Definitely over.'

'Or young.'

'Seventy is the new fifty, everybody knows that.'

'I don't. So, I'm gonna improve with age?'

'Highly unlikely.'

'Maybe you're charming with women, you know, a generational thing us young guys don't have.'

'Probably. You lot are all "Wham, bham, thank you mam" except you're unlikely to say "Thank you."'

Tawhiri laughed dismissively. He knew all about Charles from female carers at the agency. 'Money's a good leg-opener too.'

'Tawhiri! Enough of that!'

'Doesn't take much. Depends what they want.' Tawhiri stood up to his full height. 'There's a traditional Maori saying, "You don't need an ocean to sail your boat, a river will do."'

'Really? Depends on your boat. It needed an ocean to float the *QE2*.'

'I'm talking boats. Not rule Britannia liners.'

'I don't believe you.'

'Don't believe what?'

'That it's a Maori saying.'

'You're right.'

'The thing is, I understand women,' Charles said. 'You don't. You think it's all about chatting them up and buying them things. A man needs to know what makes women tick, what makes them want to be with him. You have to make them want to buy what you're selling.'

'Or make the man want to buy what the woman's selling. But Charles, you're obviously right, look at you, and look at me.' He smiled ironically. 'I'd better get on with my caring – and think on your words of wisdom, eh.'

*

'Pretty woman, walking down the street, pretty woman, the kind I like to meet.'

'You know the words!' Jasmine said in surprise.

'I know the words to all his songs.' Charles continued to sing along in a scratchy tuneless voice.

'When you going to tell me where we're going?'

'Just a drive to Ballina. If I tell, it won't be a surprise.' Charles started singing again. 'Pretty woman, stop a while, pretty woman, give your smile to me.' Charles paused to regain his breath. 'I'm thinking of a career change.'

'A singer?'

'Yes.'

'Don't. Be a brain surgeon. You'd be better at that.'

Charles continued, 'Pretty woman, look my way…'

'I'm surprised Roy Orbison's your thing,' Jasmine said.

'Best singer ever, but he wouldn't have known who was pretty and who wasn't. He was blind as a bat.'

'He wasn't. He wore dark glasses because they looked cool,' Jasmine said.

'Really? I'd better get a pair.'

'His eyesight was really bad, though, like yours. So you've got something in common, as well as both being brilliant singers.'

Charles accompanied Roy Orbison again. 'Pretty woman, say you'll staaay with me,' he croaked. 'Come with me baby, be miiiine tonight.'

Jasmine pursed her lips.

'Turn right. The secret will now unfold. Take us to Ballina RSL, driver.'

'OK, we're heading for a wild night out?'

'Too right.'

Jasmine pulled into the crowded car park, helped Charles into his wheelchair and pushed him to an auditorium overflowing with Saturday night energy. Sympathetic patrons found a space for them near a stage draped with a banner declaring, 'Roy Orbison "Reborn" starring the world's No. 1 Roy Orbison tribute star Danny Dean.'

Jasmine went off to get drinks. When she came back, her face was flushed. 'Guess who I've just seen?' She put a jug of beer down on the table with a thump.

'Roy Orbison?'

'Your daughter! Stephanie!'

'Really?'

'With Tawhiri.'

'I don't believe you.'

'Please yourself, but here they come.'

This was the first time Charles had seen Tawhiri in anything but his Cared-for uniform. He looked like a Maori totem pole. He squeezed his way between the tables towards them, a diminutive Stephanie close behind. Heads turned.

'Hello, Charles, Jasmine,' Tawhiri said, grinning down on them.

'This is a surprise, Dad.' Stephanie kissed her father.

'You can say that again,' said Charles.

'OK if we join you?' Stephanie asked.

'Our pleasure.' Charles extended a hand towards the table.

'You don't want to be a singer too do you?' Jasmine asked Tawhiri.

Tawhiri shook his head. 'No. I dance, I'll get up on stage and show you, eh? What you think, Charles? Stick my tongue out and go aaaaaah?' Tawhiri did, and everyone laughed, except those on adjacent tables, who thought they are sitting near a maniac.

'We'll do a double act. I'll sing along. Come on.' Charles moved his wheelchair as though to head to the stage.

'Don't!' Stephanie grabbed Charles and he started laughing.

'See what I've gotta put up with,' Jasmine said.

Stephanie looked at her. 'I've lived with it all my life.'

Tawhiri disappeared in the direction of the bar.

'How long's this been going on?' Charles asked Stephanie, taking a swig of beer.

'Nothing's going on. We're friends. You've got friends – well, *a* friend. I've got a number of friends.'

'I just asked. No need to bite my head off or make smart comments. Just don't let him put any of those tattoos on your face, or anywhere else.'

'Come on, children, let's play happy families,' Jasmine said.

Tawhiri returned with a jug of beer in each fist. 'We need to celebrate,' he said, pouring drinks all round.

'Agreed.' Charles raised his glass.

'OK, you can start, Charles. What should we celebrate?' Tawhiri said.

Charles puffed his cheeks out to gain time. 'Um, girls, starting with these two here.' He raised his glass.

Everyone followed. 'To girls.'

Stephanie and Jasmine looked at each other over the rim of their glasses as they drank.

'When do we become women, Dad?' Stephanie asked.

'You know what I mean, Steph.'

'I do. Indeed.'

'Never,' Jasmine said to her.

'Someone has to provide for you,' Charles replied.

Stephanie and Jasmine laughed sarcastically, and again raised their glasses – to each other.

'Jasmine's turn!' Tawhiri prompted.

The three waited as Jasmine looked around the table.

'Everyone should be true to themselves,' she finally said.

'I'll drink to that.' Charles did.

'Stephanie,' Jasmine prompted.

Stephanie had no need to gather her thoughts, 'To patience. To boys, and to the day they become men. Your turn, Tawhiri.'

'No, I'm the team leader. Exempt.'

The other three joshed him until he relented.

'Families. We should all look after our families.'

'I'll drink to that as well,' said Charles, and he did.

*

Charles was still singing 'Pretty Woman' when he got home.

Jasmine pushed him up the ramp, laughing. 'Shhh, you'll wake the neighbours.'

'Bugger the neighbours.'

Jasmine closed the door behind them. 'Let's dance.' She grabbed Charles by the wrist and spun the chair round.

The wheels squealed on the parquet floor, faster and faster, Charles at the centre, Jasmine whirling in an outer orbit.

'Pretty woman, look my way…' Charles squawked. 'Come on, Jasmine, you know the words.'

'I can't sing and dance.'

'You can if you want.'

'No!'

'Come on!'

Jasmine sang fragments, breathlessly out of tune, 'Pretty woman… I don't…'

Charles joined in. '…believe you…'

'…you're not…'

Jasmine let go and stood, blowing for air.

Charles finished the verse. '…the truth…' He clapped this hands in a discordant rhythm, then started singing again, 'Cos I need you, I'll treat you right. Come with me baby, be miiiine tonight.' He threw back his head. 'Give me the rest, Jasmine.'

'I don't know the rest.' She leaned against the kitchen bench to regain her breath. 'Where's this sudden energy come from, Charles?'

'I haven't enjoyed myself so much in years,' he panted. 'Can you believe it? Steph with that Maori. And what did he mean, our families?'

'Same as everyone else means probably. Come on, Charles, bed. I've got work in the morning.' She tweaked the back of his neck playfully as she guided the wheelchair out of the lounge room down the hall and into Charles's bedroom.

'I was having fun,' Charles said.

'And me.' She hugged him, then eased him from the wheelchair and onto the bed.

Charles stretched out and sang, 'Take care of meeee.' He started laughing. 'I love being undressed by you.'

'Who said you're gonna be undressed?'

'You're my carer, you have to…'

Jasmine stood looking down on him. She leaned over, held him teasingly by an ear and kissed him on the cheek.

Charles grabbed her arm and pulled her down on top of him. He started to laugh.

'What's funny?' Jasmine asked.

'Viagra is. The sleeping giant is awake.'

Jasmine guffawed. 'I thought you were too drunk.'

'I'm never too drunk.' He released his hold. 'Never!'

Jasmine climbed off the bed. With her back to him, she began to undress. The last garment to join the pile at her feet were the French knickers. She turned around and walked towards the bed. 'What is it you keep saying, Charles – conditions apply?'

*

Next morning, the sun was shining on the cul-de-sac below where Charles and Jasmine were at the window eating a leisurely breakfast. Charles was smiling, more to himself than to Jasmine and the rest of the world.

Jasmine gestured in the direction of the outside. 'Do you want me to tell you what the gardens in this cul-de-sac look like?' she asked.

'No. I know, more or less.'

'Can you see what they could look like?'

'What are talking about? I can see what I can see. That's it.'

'Tell me what you think the gardens could look like, as an exercise.'

'I'm not into exercise for obvious reasons.'

'A brain exercise.'

'You haven't taken up Zen Buddhism or yoga have you?'

'No. Try. Say something.'

'They're just there, like the road and the houses. I suppose they're pretty…'

'Pretty?'

'Let me finish! Pretty dull. A few hibiscus, a few other little things that I can't see properly and I wouldn't know the names of if I could, and lots of grass that Peter next door, and the rest of them, mow every Saturday morning, making a hell of a noise and stink. Then they turn the sprinklers on so they'll have to do the same thing the next weekend. That's what I see.'

'I've got a plan that would give you weekends of peace.'

'You going to shoot my neighbours? I don't think you'd get away with it.'

'I'll persuade them to use their gardens better. You know, plant them with shrubs and trees. There'll be shade, blossom. Birds.'

Charles shook his head. 'No, you won't persuade them. It's the way they like it. No trees to blow over onto the house in a storm. No branches to drop on somebody's head. No leaves in the gutters. A couple of years ago, a guy wanted a tree outside his house taken down because he said it was dangerous. Some expert greenie on the council parks department said no, it was a healthy tree. A week later, the tree blew over. It killed the guy. Not the council greenie, that would have been divine intervention, but the poor bugger who wanted it cut down.'

'Small trees. Not Eucalyptus regnans, no mountain ash.'

'How small? Trees spoil the view.'

'What of? The road? Trees are the view. I'd love to see all this changed.'

Charles screwed up his mouth in disapproval, but then said, 'All right then. But no trees on my place. You can put in a few more hibiscus.'

Before lunch, Jasmine began knocking on doors in the cul-de-sac. By late afternoon, enough people had agreed to have their gardens landscaped. Jasmine's dream was about to become reality.

Jasmine was driving into the cul-de-sac on Monday morning as Tawhiri was driving out. They stopped, side by side.

'I'm gonna plant you in all these gardens, Mr Pittosporum, small New Zealand tree that you aren't,' Jasmine said, climbing out of her ute.

'What you on about, Jasmine?'

'Trees, something to remind Charles of you when you're gone.'

'Who says I'm going?' Tawhiri waved a dismissive arm and drove off smiling as he looked in his rear mirror. Jasmine's ute was overflowing with the tools of her trade: spades, mattocks, plant hole diggers, wooden stakes – and trees.

Mounds of brown soil appeared at holes in next door's garden. Jasmine put in trees, she put in shrubs, she secured them with wooden stakes and spread mulch around their base. She watered them. Then she drove away and came back with more plants and dug more holes, planted more trees, and watered them. All day, Charles could see her vague figure labouring in the heat.

In the late afternoon, Jasmine drudged wearily into the house, showered away the sweat and dirt of the day and sat down with Charles for their evening drinks. The first garden was complete.

Charles raised his glass. 'Here's to silent Saturday mornings.'

'And beautiful gardens.'

Over the following weeks of back-breaking work, Jasmine created more new gardens in the cul-de-sac. She could visualise how they would look ten years from now. She talked to Charles about her dream. 'I could do this everywhere on the coast, create real gardens. It would make money for us. You could look after the business side, I could do the hard yakka outside, maybe employ someone to work with me. And it would stop you being bored.'

'Do you have the money to set it up?'

'The short answer's no.'

'And the long answer's no.'

'I'd need a tipper truck for starters to cart soil and trees, and the rest.'

'I'd need to buy it?'

'You'd get it back. Loads of people have moved up here from Sydney and Melbourne. Lotsa money, no imagination. They're just waiting for me to turn up.'

'Like a horticulture messiah?'

'That's it!'

'Not sure it is. But I'll sleep on it.'

He did.

'I've got nothing to lose,' he told Jasmine. 'I never thought I'd be making money out of trees.'

Charles rang Luke Little. The car salesman was surprised and delighted. Charles told him that Jasmine would be visiting him and that he, Charles, would supply the bank details to cover whatever she chose.

A week later, a new Isuzu tipper truck was parked in Charles's drive. It belonged to Jasmine. She hired a young guy, Billy, to help her with the work and they completed the remaining landscaping contracts she had signed-up in the cul-de-sac.

She wheeled Charles around one evening when the magpies were singing and the heat had gone out of the day so he could see her work close up.

'Uuum,' he said.

'What does uuum mean?'

'Just that – uuum. I've got to admit that as far as I can see they look better than before, as long as you've put in the right plants, none of the biggest in the world ones.'

'Of course. In contrast to our place – I mean, your place – which looks more like a golf fairway than a garden.'

Jasmine continued pushing the chair, explaining to Charles the specifics of each garden as they passed. She named the trees and shrubs, when they flowered and what the flowers would look like, how the flowers would smell, and how tall the trees would grow.

Charles relented under the onslaught. 'OK. OK. You win. Do my place too.'

Charles's garden was transformed into an arboretum of black matipo – and more. Hidden among them was a single mountain ash.

Each day, Jasmine was away in the truck by six thirty a.m. and not back until late afternoon, exhausted. Happy. She and Charles entered the culinary world of frozen supermarket dinners. Tawhiri looked after Charles morning and night. Charles looked after the books, happy to be making money again.

*

Jasmine bought all her tree stock from her old boss, Hunter. Not because of loyalty. It gave her great pleasure being his customer because, as everyone knows, the customer is always right. Hunter smiled every time she drove through the gate. He seemed really pleased to see her. Jasmine smiled back.

'What can I do for you today, Jasmine?' he'd ask.

He never said anything like that when she worked for him. It was always, get this, get that, do this do that, you're too slow, you sent the wrong order. She never sent a wrong order, he did, and blamed someone else, usually her.

Being a customer put her in a position of power. She would wait until Hunter had loaded the truck then change her mind and decide she had ordered too many of something or other and not enough of something else, usually mountain ash. Hunter would have to off-load half the truck, wheel the unwanted plants back to their place and fetch and load the new ones. It was hard work, as Jasmine well new. She and Billy would stand and watch.

Jasmine knew the price of every plant. There was no way her old boss could rip her off. She could drive down the price of everything. She was, after all, a regular customer who had a growing business, forgive the pun. Hunter did not want her to buy from a giant rival nursery that had opened on an industrial estate, nor one of the small rivals about to be choked out of business. Jasmine could have bought the plants from any of the other nursery of course and not given Hunter her business, but she weighed things up and decided that the pleasure of giving him the run around outweighed any satisfaction he might get from counting his money at the end of the day.

*

As Charles was being wheeled into the bathroom for his morning shower, Tawhiri said, 'Jasmine seems very pleased with her new business.' He eased Charles onto his stool and turned on the shower. 'You're a lucky man, eh?'

'Not too bloody hot. You nearly lobstered me yesterday,' Charles said.

'Yeah. One happy woman. She goes off singing every morning,' Tawhiri said.

'Lucky for her she earns a living growing things not singing about them. But yes, she's happy. More jobs come in every week. I'm busy as.' Charles spluttered from beneath the shower. 'It's a – what? A win-win situation. That's what the Labor pollies usually say when they've shafted some small businessman. But this is a real win-win.'

Tawhiri left Charles washed and polished sitting at the window with a laptop on the small table. He felt how lucky he was that Jasmine knew her job. Between them, they would grow it into a nice little business. Charles made a mental note to use the grow pun with Jasmine.

*

She worked hard and she worked long but one night she was late coming home. Charles became tired of waiting and opened a beer. He sat slowly drinking, looking down the drive and along the cul-de-sac to the main road. Twilight turned to dusk, dusk too dark. The street lights came on. He could hear the fruit bats drifted low overhead as they set out for the night's foraging.

45

Still Jasmine did not come. Charles phoned her mobile but it was switched off. He phoned Stephanie but got voicemail and didn't leave a message.

The feeling of unease in his belly turned to anxiety. He rang the police. There had been a serious accident involving a number of vehicles outside Ballina. Charles gave the Isuzu's rego. They told him to ring back later when they would have more information.

He sat and sweated. The truck on its back, unseen at the bottom of a deep gully, wheels still slowly turning, Jasmine hanging by her seatbelt, face veiled with blood. The truck, crushed against a tree by the side of the road, Jasmine impaled on the steering wheel. He could not get the images out of his mind. He even said a prayer for her safety.

He rang the police again. Jasmine's rego did not match any of the vehicles involved.

Charles wanted the police to start a search but the woman officer politely told him that a partner who was a few hours late arriving home was not a missing person. Even if they did not come home all night, they were not a missing person.

What if she did not come home all night, just showed up in the morning? Such things happened. He took a sip of his now warm beer then pushed it aside and got a cold can from the fridge. He sat sipping and looking out of the window. He fell asleep in his chair. When he awoke, crickets were chirping outside in the darkness. His neck was stiff and painful.

He wheeled his chair down the hallway and into the guest room. In the pale wash of light from the street lamp, he could see the unmade bed but nothing else indicated that anyone had been there. The tops of the bedside tables which were usually cluttered with combs and other women things were bare. Charles opened a drawer. It was empty. The French knickers were gone. He tried the other drawer. Empty. He slid aside the wardrobe door. No green silk dress was hanging there, only the faint smell of musky perfume and a row of empty coat hangers swinging slightly with the vibrations from the opened door.

Charles felt like he had fallen off a cliff.

He waited.

He talked to no one for days.

It wasn't the money. It was the rejection.

After a week, he received an email: 'Charles, sorry to do it that way. I tried not to hurt you. Each of us had something the other wanted and we did a deal. In your businessman's way of thinking, we both found a buyer, the buyers paid a price. And, as you said in the start, conditions applied. We had some good times. Don't forget to water the trees. Jasmine.'

That was the last contact Charles had with her.

Almost.

Six months later, he was in a taxi on his way to dinner, stopped at a red light on the way into Ballina. An Isuzu truck pulled up alongside. The back was full of young trees.

Jasmine?

Charles squinted across. Next to Jasmine in the cab was a teenage girl. She had the same broad features as Jasmine. Her left hand, which was hanging on the outside of the door, was large for a girl, and strong looking. Her hair was the same colour as Jasmine's, but cut short. Jasmine turned and said something to the girl and smiled. The girl touched Jasmine on the shoulder. The lights changed.

They were gone.

The words mother and daughter leapt into Charles's mind. Now he understood Friday nights.

*

Charles arrived at the Indian restaurant early. The taxi driver wheeled him into the air-conditioned interior where the manager, a tall imposing Sikh with a long beard and bright green turban, welcomed him with a flourish. Waiters scurried to clear a path for the wheelchair and the manager led the way to a table. Charles wriggled himself onto a seat. A Visit to India was one of the best restaurants on the north coast. The sweet smell of curry and cooking meat infused the darkened narrow dining room. Charles liked the restaurant because it was quiet and had secluded booths, velvet walls and murals of ludicrously nubile half naked women. Soft Indian music played in the background.

Charles wore chinos matched with a dark blue long-sleeve cotton shirt. On his feet he had light tan plaited leather Italian shoes. His hair was combed, his chin shaved and he smelled of jasmine-scented after shave.

He ordered a beer and a bottle of white wine which chinked pleasantly in its bucket of ice as the waiter set it on the table. Charles sat and sipped his beer and waited. His date would arrive in few minutes.

Her name was Bianca. She was Polish.

But at that moment Bianca was not the woman on his mind.

Superman

People often ask me, 'Where do you work?' I tell them at home. Which isn't true.

A couple of blocks away from where I live there is a phone booth on the side of a dead-end road, not the sort where Superman slipped into his blue body suit before zooming off to save the world for the American way and law and order. It's one of those old-style Sydney affairs, with the top half glassed-in and the bottom half open to the elements. When it rains, your head is dry but you feet are wet. Whoever designed it got it half right – the top.

I work there because my previously peaceful room overlooking an old wooden house and garden next door is now a construction site. Once the builders had knocked the house down, they started to dig a hole through solid sandstone towards the centre of the earth then began erecting a twenty-storey block of flats from which there'll be views of other twenty-storey blocks of flats. Probably investment properties for politicians. The job was going to be complete in two years. That was three years ago.

But back to my new workplace. Because everyone has a mobile phone these days, no one uses the phone box. You could even live in if you didn't mind sleeping standing up.

Each morning, I tuck my laptop under my arm and head to the office. I balance the computer on the coin box and start tapping away. Initially, I found standing pretty tiring, but as this is now the preferred method of working in progressive offices that are conscious of their employees' health, I persevered.

I have nothing against health. It's great, but I'm not much into exercise, like pedalling madly on a gym bike that goes nowhere and leaves you knackered; or a sweaty run that ends up back where you started after you've been attacked by packs of dogs or tripped over a kerb and broken your arm.

I enter my workplace at nine a.m. and start writing my latest novel where I left off. It's going well, I have to admit. A real page-turner. I reckon it will make me famous. I have a short list of the major publishers who are accepting unsolicited manuscripts. It's very short. But I'm sure I'll crack one of them.

As workplaces go, it's not the best. In summer, I cook; now winter's starting, it's cold. Particularly on the feet. But there's a coffee shop close by called the Hole in the Wall where I can warm up. There's also a spectacular-looking waitress, dark hair, dark complexion, Middle Eastern or Jewish. Could even be Indian. The barista calls her Alaska. I wonder if it means what I think it means. It sounds better than being called Kosciuszko, which is cold too. If I work hard and meet my daily word quota, I'll be finished before the sun slides behind the tall buildings. By then, I'll have been standing here a few hours.

Maybe being uncomfortable is a good way to write – keeps you on edge, helps you create characters that are like that, not complacent, not the smug middle-class characters obsessed with relationships that inhabit contemporary novels. I don't really care who's screwing whom, or whether they've found their identity, or decided to come out, or are non-binary, neutrois, gender-fluid. If that's what people want to write about, fine by me, but it's boring.

This morning I'm rattling along. My protagonist, Chloe – you have a better chance of success if the main character is a woman – has befriended Faheem, an asylum-seeker from Sudan. Asylum-seekers are big news right now. He is afraid his application will be rejected. She thinks he has fallen in love with her but she also thinks he might be using her to get a permanent resident visa.

I might make him gay, and pretending to be in love with her. That would make it even more interesting. She could be lesbian, in which case he'd be wasting his time either way. I think. If I do that, I can pitch it at the LGBTQIA community. He might even be Aboriginal, locked up in the white criminal justice system for some minor offence. Chloe could thrown her energies into a campaign waged by his local community to have him freed.

So it is, in a way, about relationships, but in the context of what's going on in the wider world – war, racism, cruelty, fear of the other, rotten governments, that sort of thing.

I'm writing a really tense scene when I hear a metallic tapping on the glass. I hate being disturbed when my creative juices are flowing.

As I turn round, a girl says, 'I want to make a phone call.'

This is the first time it's happened in nearly a year.

'I'm writing a novel,' I tell her.'

'In a phone box?'

'Looks like it,eh.'

'Why?'

'It's a long story.'

'Literally?'

'Of course it's literary, it's a novel.'

She looks like my character Chloe, or the way I imagine her, slight, beneath red fleece jacket and jeans. Pretty.

'Can you wait a few minutes till I finish this really important chapter?'

'No. It's urgent.'

'Can't you just wait five minutes?'

'No.'

She knows her own mind. I pick up my laptop and empty styrofoam coffee cup and step outside. She squeezes past me, takes the phone off the hook, puts coins in the slot, dials, then hunches over the handset and begins to talk earnestly.

I try to eavesdrop but all I can hear is a blurred angry gabble. Once in a while, she stops talking and listens, elbows on the coin box, hunched over, concentrating intently.

I'm cold.

I feel like tapping on the window like she did, but remind myself that I was in there for nearly three uninterrupted hours before she arrived. Fair's fair. But being fair doesn't keep me warm as I stand on the gritty footpath with the wind around my neck, my laptop under my arm and the empty coffee cup still in my hand. I try to keep the next chapters in my head and progress the story but the plot is soon as cold and empty as the coffee cup.

The girl inside is leaning against the coin box and looks set for the day.

I give up and head for the Hole in the Wall. I sit down at a small table in the corner of the crowded fuggy room and open up my laptop. It pings into life but that is as far as it goes. My characters have abandoned me, walked off, gone to do whatever they do when they aren't with me. I'm stuffed. My day's ruined.

And Alaska isn't here either.

I get a coffee, sip and brood. My creative tide is on its way out and there is nothing I can do. I could try a long walk but that would tire me rather than inspire me. I look around the coffee shop for ideas. Everyone is deep in conversation with their mobile phones, and some of them with each other.

The door opens and the girl from the phone box steps into the warmth, her arms wrapped around her thin body, the tip of her nose and cheeks pink from the cold. Part of me wants to cuddle her to get her warm, another part reminds me that she killed my creative process at its daily peak.

She looks around for somewhere to sit. There is only one empty seat, next to me. She stands for a while, hoping someone will get up and go. They don't.

Eventually she walks over. 'Is that seat taken?' She nods in the direction of the obviously empty chair.

I am tempted to say, 'Yeah.' But I say, 'No.'

She sits down. I try not to look at her, which is hard when someone is sitting a metre in front of you. She has taken off her beanie and her short-cropped hair gives her the look of a pixie.

She doesn't try to avoid me but looks me in the eye. 'I'm Ember.'

'I'm Tim,' I say after a moment's hesitation.

'What's your novel about?'

I wonder whether she's humouring me because she thinks I'm mad. I'm not.

'Do you really want to know?'

'That's why I asked.'

I like telling people about what I'm writing. In fact, once I get going, I can't stop. They get the whole story, for free. But I control myself and tell her a short version.

'Aren't you jumping on the bandwagon, you know, about asylum-seekers and gay people, without any understanding?'

What a hide. 'Of course not.'

'What have you had published?'

I hate that question. 'This'll be my first.'

She smiles. Not exactly patronising but somewhere between that and encouraging.

'What do you like to read?' I ask.

'I can't read.'

'Bullshit.'

'My mum thinks that only the spoken word is pure. The written word is tarnished by contact with the human hand. She home-schooled me. Us. My three sisters as well. She's not keen on new technology, my mum.'

'Writing's not exactly new,' I point out.

'Other things as well.'

'How did she teach anything?' I try to keep disbelief and derision out of my voice.

'She talked. We talked. That's what people did before they could write.'

'That's true. What about?'

'Nature. History. Harmony. Kindness.'

'But you're a woman now. How come you still can't read?'

'It's catching on, the purity of only the spoken word. There are more followers.'

I am about to tell her that it's the twenty-first century and she needs to read to know what's going on and I'll teach her, but the noisy coffee shop suddenly goes silent. I look towards the door. You are not going to believe this. Superman has walked in. Over his arms he is carrying a crushed business suit, a shirt and tie, and in his hand a pair of dress shoes with black socks dangling from them. He looks tatty and tired. Nothing like the comic book hero.

Ember turns to look at what I am staring at. 'What a strange guy, who is he?' she says in disbelief.

'Superman.'

'Never heard of him.'

'No, you wouldn't.'

For some reason, of all the people in the café he catches my eye and walks towards us.

On the way, he picks up a stool that has been vacated. 'Do you mind?' He sets the stool down close to the table.

'No,' Ember and I say in unison.

'No need for me to introduce myself, I suppose,' Superman says in a tired voice.

We introduce ourselves.

As he is about to sit, I notice that his body suit is baggy at the bum. He's like a kid whose nappy is full and coming adrift. His blue, skin-tight T-shirt isn't skin-tight any more and there are holes at the elbow. The big 'S' on his chest is coming unstuck.

'Cell phones have ended my career. I'm finished,' he says wearily in a soft American drawl. 'Nobody builds proper phone booths any more. I can't get changed in a transparent perspex bubble. It would be wrong. I'd embarrass my fellow Americans.'

'What about public toilets?' Ember says. 'There's one here.'

'I couldn't leave my suit, it would be stolen.'

I don't think anyone would steal his gear these days.

'Those old booths had special qualities. They were shipped all over the world by the US government. Just for me,' Superman says with pride, sticking out his chest, which actually isn't up to much.

He eases his belt a little and sinks back. He's a bit thick around the waist. 'I'm the only one who can operate the unique locking system,' he explains.

The three of us sit in silence. The rest of the coffee shop customers have stopped talking and are watching us. That is, they are watching him, Superman. Some are on their mobile phones excitedly telling people what's happening. Others are bent double and creeping up on us, smartphones poised. They seem to think they are in the jungle and no can see them.

I don't know what to say next. Superman has his elbows on his knees, slumped forward. He is going grey at the temple.

Ember, who should be the expert on the spoken word, is thinking, not talking.

People are taking selfies with Superman.

A tall guy with a black shovel beard wants to know, 'What happened to Su-per-maaan?' and laughs.

A young guy asks, 'You making an ad for antidepressant pills? Are you the before or after image?'

The Superman I knew would have blown these two out of the room with one puff.

Eventually, Ember stands. 'Superman, maybe you should put on your other clothes. You might feel better. Come on, I'll show you where the loo is.'

Superman looks up. He adjusts the cloak on his shoulders. He licks his finger, wipes it on the back of the unstuck 'S' and tries to re-stick it. After a moment, he follows Ember obediently. His clothes are draped over his arm, his red boots are tucked under his elbow.

'I'll tell Lois Lane on you,' spade beard calls out as he takes photos of the retreating pair.

With Ember and Superman out of sight, the patrons go back to their phones.

I order another coffee and wait. The barista tells me that Alaska isn't coming in today because she's off on some course.

Ten, fifteen minutes. I get up and go out to the toilet to look for Superman and Ember. I open the door. Superman's grubby red cloak is hanging from a hook. On the floor by the side of the toilet bowl are his knee-length boots, his blue body suit and his baggy red Y-fronts.

I dash through the kitchen and out into the back lane. I glimpse Amber and Superman as they disappear round a corner hand-in-hand at a run.

'Ember! Ember, don't!' I yell.

Why is she doing this? She doesn't know who he is. He's a fictional character and she can't read. He'll just disappear.

What a lousy, rotten day this is.

I go back to the café and retrieve my laptop. The patrons are all back on their phones.

I have second thoughts. Maybe it's not a lousy, rotten day. I can use everything that's happened for my story. I'll have to pitch it to different readers, not the LGBTQIA community nor those who worry about asylum-seekers. I'm not sure who the new readers will be, but it'll come to me.

I hurry out of the coffee shop, one hand on my head, hanging on to the ideas that are racing round in there. I walk quick as I can to the dead-end road and my office.

The phone booth is not there. In its place is a glistening new, transparent half-bubble minimalist thing. There's isn't even a coin box to rest my laptop on.

I'm devastated.

I retreat to the Hole in the Wall clutching my work in progress.

The bastard barista was lying about Alaska. She is there. She smiles at me and brings over my coffee. She's remembered what I like.

The barista glares. He's jealous.

She's not Alaska-cold at all.

I open my laptop and start typing.

The Wake

There was the death, the funeral and the wake. It wasn't a big wake as wakes go.

Alison had rung me to say Mark had died. I hadn't seen either of them since I visited him in hospital two years ago. That was still as vivid in my mind as the day it happened, and as disturbing. She said she understood that it had been a confronting experience.

Alison had remained a devoted partner, sitting every day by the side of his bed, awaiting the inevitable.

I tried to make excuses to avoid the wake. She pleaded with me, said it would help her move on from the whole terrible thing and give me the opportunity to say farewell to a comrade regardless of what had happened. She wouldn't take no for an answer.

I no longer have a car, and since it happened, I don't travel on trains any more, so I took a bus to her flat, which was near a station. I nearly got off at every stop to go back home but regrettably I didn't.

I hesitated at the door of the flat, my finger hovering in front of the bell. The sound of muffled voices came from the other side. I could still have changed my mind, rung Alison later, told her I'd had a heart attack or broken my leg or something. I didn't, I pressed the bell instead.

Alison opened the door. She'd put on a huge amount of weight since I'd last seen her. She smiled briefly. 'Thanks for coming. He'd appreciate it, if you know what I mean.'

I nodded. She led me in and introduced me to the first person we met, Jessica, who was standing sipping a glass of mineral water. Jessica in turn introduced me to two young men, Benjamin and David, who were standing, limply by, doing nothing.

I asked how she had known Mark.

'He was my husband once.'

That was a shock – I didn't even know he'd been married. Alison said the two skinny, slack-mouthed young men were their sons, another shock. They didn't look anything like Mark, who'd been all bone and muscle with eyes that glared rather than looked. These two seemed embarrassed to be alive. I could see what had attracted Mark to their mother, though: long blonde hair and a still slender figure which she was hiding under a plain, floppy dress. I wondered why he had never mentioned them when life was normal and he could talk and did talk, lots. I wondered why they'd split up. Too much politics? Other women? Both? Neither.

Another surprise was being introduced to a Catholic priest, Father McMahon. I'd never heard of him either. Mark was an atheist. He said religion stopped people thinking. Alison was an atheist too. He'd been able to keep religion out of his life but not out of his death. What was a Catholic priest doing there? It could only have been Alison's call, maybe one of those lapsed Catholic reversions, a kind of last-minute insurance policy just in case. Father McMahon was in his fifties, unkempt flyaway white hair, and talking quietly. He shook my hand then moved on.

The flat was unlikely to be featured in a home beautiful magazine. There was a mishmash of old furniture. Books spilled from shelves along one wall. Tolstoy's *Anna Karenina* was open on a small table as though it had been put down when the doorbell rang. Through the window I could see red-brick blocks of flats, TV aerials, sat-dishes and a concrete car park.

A table was spread with nibbles, dips, Leb bread, mineral water and orange juice. I looked around for proper drinks but there was no sign of any. Mark had been too much of a fitness fanatic to drink alcohol but I knew that Alison liked a glass or two.

I wondered how long before I could decently slip away. I thought of telling her I was crook. She was talking to a white-haired dumpy woman in her sixties who was licking hummus from her fingers and nodding her head earnestly. I wanted to be anywhere but there. I had made the wrong decision.

I slipped into the little kitchen in the hope of finding a beer or something in the fridge. Father McMahon was there. He had either found what I was looking for or brought it with him and was pouring whisky into a glass. He lifted the bottle in my direction in a silent question. I nodded and he reached up into a wall cupboard and took out another glass without looking. He was obviously familiar with the kitchen.

'To a good man,' he said, raising his glass.

'A good man,' I replied.

'You knew Mark a long time…'

I wasn't sure whether it was a question or a statement.

'How did you meet?'

'Politics.'

'Ah, yes, like most others it seems.' He cupped his glass in both hands and gazed down at the whisky.

I returned the question and it hung there for some moments.

'Sometimes, regardless of what people believe or think they don't believe, they need to reach out for help in times of crisis.'

I took a sip of my whisky and waited for a sermon.

'I visit at the hospital where Mark was and I got talking to Alison one day in the garden. She was suffering. Her commitment to Mark was true Christian love. Taking your own life is a terrible thing, a sin. And when the attempt fails, like in Mark's case, and it leaves body and mind shattered, the suffering goes on, for everyone.'

He seemed to expect me to respond but I didn't and he went on in a low gravelly voice, 'Alison and I became friends. She would talk to me about the ordeal. Most of their friends couldn't handle what had happened.' MacMahon took another sip. 'From what she told me, Mark's suicide attempt seemed out of character.' He shook his head slowly side to side.

'I guess none of us know how we'll react to a crisis,' I said. 'Did you talk to him?'

'I tried,' Father McMahon said.

'Did he make any sense?'

'No.'

'Never?'

'No, never.'

'Same with me.' I didn't mention that I hadn't seen him in a long time, but he probably knew.

'He'd get angry and stick out those poor stumps of legs and hands and make terrible moaning noises. The neurosurgeon said it was impossible to know whether he understood anything. But I think he did.'

'Why?' I asked, trying to keep the concern out of my voice.

'His eyes, you could see something there, trapped.'

Neither of us said anything for a while then Father McMahon downed his drink. 'I'd better circulate.' He slipped the bottle into the cupboard and left.

I took it out a couple of minutes later and poured another one, large. As a Christian gentleman, I didn't think Father McMahon would mind. I put the bottle back and followed him into the other room.

Alison came over, took me by the arm and led me to a group who were chatting together. It always seems strange at funerals and wakes when people behave as though they are at a party. The dead person, the reason they are there, is gone, so they concentrate on those who are there, the living.

A small, slim young woman in her twenties with a squeaky voice was Alison's niece, Zoe, an aspiring actor who had been in a couple of TV soapies and was talking about how exciting it was meeting the stars and being in the studio at Channel 10. Her boyfriend, Vince, a tall guy with a mop of dark hair, kept smiling at her approvingly. A fourth in the group was Kelly, her mother and Alison's sister, a tough, no-nonsense nurse in her forties who I'd met years ago.

They were there to support Alison, respecting her three-year vigil at Mark's bedside. Maybe they, like me, had been stupid enough to take Mark's advice. Others who had done the same were noticeable because they weren't there. Like me, they too would have felt murderous to start with, then horrified, now perhaps relieved that his suffering was over, and maybe feeling guilty at not visiting him.

I made my way over to Mark's ex, Jessica, who was standing with her two sons. I told her Mark and I had been political collaborators. She smiled, ironically perhaps, and said she had seen me at one of the public meetings. I was flattered. Benjamin and David muttered something in response then focused their eyes on the middle distance, which in Alison's small flat wasn't very far. The last few years must have been hard for them. I wondered whether they had visited him regularly in hospital or whether the sight of him was too much for them as well.

'It's sad, but best that it's all over,' I said by way of consolation. I'm not sure it was the right thing to say. I wondered how it had affected the two sons, whether their silence was an outcome of it or whether it was normal adolescent behaviour.

'We didn't see each other very much after we'd split up,' Jessica said. I visited him in hospital but that was hard, as you well know. Alison said he always recognised her, and I think he knew me, but how would you know? My church helped me cope, helped us cope,' she said, indicating her sons.

Benjamin and David looked like examples of not coping.

'Hillsong's far more than the media shows, all that singing and arm waving. People have been wonderful to me.'

I didn't know why she felt the need to say that, maybe assuming my thoughts on such issues were the same as Mark's. I wondered whether she had found God after the bust-up or before, or whether their differences on religion had led to it.

'Do you know anyone else here?' I asked.

'Alison's sister Kelly and her niece, Zoe. They're all mad, including Alison, particularly Alison.'

I didn't want to pursue that in front of Benjamin and David, then I realised that they were no longer there. Some signal, unseen by me, had passed between mother and sons and they were out of it.

'In what way are they mad?'

'They don't have a grip on reality.'

I thought that was a strange observation for a born-again happy clapper. 'In what way?'

'They'd all believed that Mark would make money for them by investing in some IT scheme he'd been told about. It was a fluke that he made money. He knew nothing about investment.'

She was right there.

'Isn't that greed rather than madness? Did you follow his advice?'

'I invested in Jesus and the Church,' Jessica said.

'Good returns?'

'Bountiful.' She smiled.

'I lost everything, every dollar,' I told her.

'I know.'

'Does that make me mad too?'

She smiled quizzically over the rim of her glass of mineral water.

I'd had enough of this Mark talk, I wanted out. I told her I was going to make my farewells with Alison.

Alison gave me a hug and said we must get together soon. I agreed, knowing it was never going to happen.

It was raining outside. Standing at a windblown wet bus stop quickly dilutes a couple of shots of whisky. I was only metres from the railway station and shelter but I couldn't muster the courage to go there.

After a few minutes, a car stopped beside me, a window slid down and Jessica leaned across. 'Want a lift?'

Did I ever. I slid in beside her, wiped the rain off my face with my hands and thanked her. I told her where to and she said it wasn't far out of her way.

'Mark could charm people,' she said after a couple of minutes.

'Don't I know it. Don't we all know it.'

'I didn't want to stay for the eulogies. Nice words would have been said about him, true no doubt. But they would have ignored the elephant in the flat,' Jessica said.

'Isn't that what always happens?'

'True. But this was a particularly big elephant.' She stopped at a pedestrian crossing, then continued what she'd been thinking as she drove on. 'Why did he throw himself under a train? He lost his money, so did you and other friends who acted on his advice. Everyone was angry with him, but to kill yourself because of it?' She shook her head.

She was still pondering the question after three years. Not satisfied with the official answers?

'Losing his own money wasn't why he did it. It was his friends losing their money that broke him,' I said.

'I know.'

We drove the rest of the way in silence and when we pulled up outside my place I invited her in for a cup of tea. I was surprised when she said yes. It is not much of a place, my home, even smaller than Alison's studio flat. I have a cupboard for a kitchen, a shoebox for a bedroom, and another room, which the literary-gifted estate agent had described, without any awareness of irony, as a sunroom. The next block of flats was about four metres away. I cleared a space for Jessica at the folding table and put the kettle on before going into the bedroom and shedding my wet clothes. There was plenty of beer in the fridge but I was sure she wouldn't want one.

'I had a nice house once. And a lovely wife,' I said, as I poured two mugs of tea.

'I'm sorry.'

'No reason to be. Money is glue. Without glue, lots of things come unstuck. And, like you said, he had charm. He talked us into a sure thing. It was against what most of us believed in but we couldn't resist the chance to set ourselves up, buy time to do what we really wanted to do, like change the world.'

She sipped her tea. This was better than the wake. I liked her face and the slenderness of her body. She was direct about what she thought. Pity about Hillsong.

I was surprised how quickly it happened, that it happened at all. I touched her hand across the table and she did not withdraw. We sat looking at each other, then I stood, holding her hand, and drew her towards me. She was weightless but I could feel her body through her thin dress. We stood like that, holding each other gently, then with increasing intensity until I led her into the shoebox where I slept – I was glad I'd made the bed before leaving that afternoon.

It was as though neither of us had drunk sex for a long time.

After, she lay in my arms and I teased strands of hair from her face. And we talked.

Inevitably, we returned to Mark and his death. There was no escaping it. His ghost was always there, intruding. No matter if you thought he'd been shut out of the room, he was present, behind the door, under the bed, in the wardrobe.

'Suicide travels alone,' Jessica whispered, her lips close to my ear, her body and legs pressed tight against me.

I wanted to say, let's not talk about it, but I felt some kind of responsibility toward here and instead I said, 'Do you mean we'd abandoned him before the attempt? After the attempt? Or when we'd lost money?'

It was a long time before she answered. 'Some people stayed with him till the end.'

'Like Alison?'

'That's not what I mean.'

I released my arms and she rolled away then swung her legs off the bed. She sat, crying, her shoulders hunched and shaking.

I reached out to comfort her but stopped short and let my hand rest on the bed. What was she getting at? My guts tightened.

'I guess most of us couldn't face what he'd done, we couldn't bear to look at him in hospital, with bits of him missing, and his brain a scrambled mess. Nothing like the man who had been our friend.' I stopped speaking, and waited for her to respond but she sat quietly crying.

'I always meant to go see him, but didn't,' I offered by way of an excuse. 'Alison was the only one who stayed with him all those months.'

I didn't say, you were once his wife, what did you do? I was sure I didn't have to.

Eventually, she turned round and looked up at me. 'What do you think happened?'

It was a chilling question. 'I know what happened. Everyone knows what happened.' I got off the bed and rammed my legs into my pants and pulled on my shirt. 'It was hard to accept. But it's not a question of thinking what happened. We all know, Mark threw himself under a train. The police said so. I was at the inquest. You were at the inquest. Alison was at the inquest.'

'Who saw him do it? There's no CCTV evidence. No witnesses.'

'No one had to see, the results were obvious.'

'The results of him going under the train were obvious, that's as far as the inquest could say.' Jessica was silent for a moment, then she said, 'What happened before that?'

I didn't like what was going on here. What was she saying? I went into the kitchen. Jessica followed. She stood behind me as I looked out of the window over the red rooftops.

Why had I invited her in?

'Do you think he was alone?' she asked.

'Of course he was. Or it wouldn't have happened. People don't take a mate along to watch them suicide.'

'A mate? What if Mark thought he was with a mate, one of the few who had stood by him? One he could talk to. What if that person was no longer a mate, but was very, very angry. What if that person had lost everything, wife, home, money. What if in a moment of resentment the friend snapped…and did something? Wasn't that it?' her voice from behind my shoulder was sharp, inquisitorial.

That's when I gave in, I guess. I couldn't turn round to face her, but a gush of words came out of me and along with them a feeling of deep relief. 'He was full of remorse, begging forgiveness, said he'd find a way to pay us all back,' I told her. 'He was pathetic. Really. The macho guy begging to be forgiven. I got angry and pushed him in the chest. He stepped back in surprise. I pushed him again. He didn't retaliate. He could have flattened me but all the fight had long gone from him. I pushed him again and he stepped back to avoid me. Neither of us had realised we were on the edge of the platform. He fell onto the tracks just as a train was going past. It was late. No one else was around. I panicked and ran.'

Jessica looked at me, her mouth tight as a trap that had been sprung. Her eyes were filled with satisfaction – and hate. She hugged her skinny body under the flimsy dress and walked quietly out of the door.

That was yesterday. I've sat here ever since, waiting and thinking of how insistent Alison was that I went to the wake; how the first person she introduced me to was Jessica; how Jessica's sons disappeared suddenly, leaving us alone.

What a coincidence she saw me waiting for a bus while she was driving in the opposite direction to where she lived.

And how easy it was to get her into bed. I don't know a lot about wholesome happy clappers, but I don't thing they're into casual sex. I could be wrong of course.

Looking back, I realise it was her who got *me* into bed.

Maybe in those three long years of sitting by Mark's bed, Alison had been able to interpret some of his grunts and roars.

Maybe Mark wasn't as brain dead as I and the neurologists thought. Father McMahon claimed he saw light in Mark's eyes.

I'm waiting for the sound of police sirens, for flashing blue lights in the street below, for the door to be smashed in.

I don't even have a beer in the fridge.

The Woman in the Photograph

'Guess who I've found. Annie. Our Little Annie, except she's not little any more and she's not Annie, she's Leanne. Seems that Annie isn't good enough for her any more. There's a photo of her in the *Tele*. She's getting into a flash car. Her hair's blonde and it must have been windy because it's blowing all over the place. It's beautiful hair. Musta cost a bomb. Have you got the paper there? Have a look at page three.

'Found it? Good. She's grown up a good-looker, hasn't she? A real beauty. Amazing. You can only see her in profile but there's no doubt it's her. It was taken outside the court, just across from state parliament. She looks important and smart, getting into a car. I can't tell what make it is, probably a Beemer, or maybe a Daimler. Not a Subaru wagon, that's for sure.

'Notice the man's hand in the photo, holding the door open for her? You can't see the whole person, just the hand with a big ring and a fancy wristwatch. Everything very swish. Tells you the sort of circles she's moving in, eh. A big change to how she looked at home. She was such a skinny kid with little tits just starting to grow, you'd remember. Now she's a gorgeous woman with big tits, isn't she…

'You're right, I agree. I bet she's had a boob job. I wouldn't. You either have tits or you don't. You have what God gave you.

'I bet she wears silk underwear now, not Bonds cotton knickers. Where does the money for that sort of thing come from, I wonder? I could have a guess.

'What did you say? I agree, that would be my guess too. But hey, here's something I hadn't noticed, a man's reflection in the window glass. He's stretching forward. It must be his hand in the photo holding open the door. Do you see?

'The paper describes her as a witness leaving court. I'm gonna go along there tomorrow, check it out, find what the sordid details are. I could take some of those old photos we have of her. She wouldn't want anybody to see them, could be well worth while… What was that? No, I won't. I'm in the station, be home in less than an hour.'

*

He's a vain pig, although I didn't use to think so. He was never handsome. But he was strong. The sort of man who'd protect you. That's what it seemed in the early days. I was young.

There's times when I'd like to kill him. Particularly when he smiles, like now, standing in the witness box, pretending to be all decent and respectable. What's the saying? 'Clothes make the man.' He's wearing black, as usual. A suit. But he still has to have a T-shirt on instead of a proper shirt with a tie, black of course, tight across his chest to show his muscles. Which makes him look less the businessman he's pretending to be and more what he is.

His smile's the most frightening thing about him because I know it can disappear faster than you can wink. Smiling's not his natural state. Just above that smiling mouth there's those eyes. They never smile, just bore right into you. I'm terrified even here in court with people all around, the cops, the judge, the public. They're only here for now, but he's around all the time.

He stands there full of confidence and contempt. Contempt for the lawyers, the cops, the whole court. The contempt's just beneath the surface. But I can see it, like a river flowing deep and fast. The only way you can tell something is going on beneath the surface is by the slight movement on top, glaring eyes, tightening of the mouth.

He's got his hands in front of him on the witness box. His big gold wristwatch stands out like a Kings Cross neon. It's the only bling he has. Although I can't tell from here, I know that his fingers have black hair all over them. So do the backs of his hands. Those hands are hard, palms and knuckles.

He answers the questions of the prosecutor with such calm sincerity. I almost believe him myself.

When we came in this morning, his lawyer handed me yesterday's newspaper. There's a photo on page three. We're getting into the car outside the court. You can only really see part of me. I don't look all that good. My hair's a mess. You can just see his hand, as though he was controlling everything. Like a puppeteer.

Yesterday was horrible. I thought it was never going to end, standing up there for hours answering questions. He'd gone over the story with me so many times, that he never received any money from me and all the rest of it but I was still afraid I'd get it wrong, forget some of the facts or get dates or times mixed up. My mind went blank. I've been in the witness box before, but it was never as serious as this, just magistrates.

When I was up there yesterday, something happened that frightened me – I nearly told the truth. It sounds funny put that way. But I almost told them everything about the whole dealings, to hell with protecting him, or me, just the truth. Then I thought of his eyes and I was too scared. No matter how long he might be sent down for, he'll get out one day and find me, or someone will do it for him while he's inside.

One of the young coppers keeps looking at me across the court-room. He can't take his eyes off me. I winked at him earlier and he blushed. A copper that blushes! He's very sweet-looking for a cop, and very young, younger than me.

The hearing drags on. At lunchtime, I go to a coffee shop a few minutes' walk away. It's full of legal types in gowns, men and women, and boring-looking people in suits. I get a cappuccino and find a table tucked in a corner and sit facing the window, spooning chocolate off the top. I half hope the young copper will be there but he's not. In a few minutes, I'm walled in by bodies of people from the courts. It feels secure and warm with everybody around me. I close my eyes and sip the coffee. Time passes without me realising.

When I open my eyes again, most of the people have gone and my hands are still resting on the cup.

There is just one person, sitting at the next table, reading a newspaper spread out in front of her face. The photograph of me getting into the car is on the page facing me. I still have my copy, the one the lawyer gave me and I feel self-conscious seeing myself up there, then I realise it's yesterday's paper. It has to be with that photo.

Why is this woman next to me reading yesterday's paper? I pick up another newspaper from the table next to me and check the date. I'm right. She is reading yesterday's paper.

There is no movement from the woman, neither the hands, the paper, nor what I can see of her head.

I sit watching, a knot growing tighter and tighter in my stomach.

Eventually, the paper is slowly lowered. The woman looks at me and smiles. I nearly faint with shock.

'Mother!' After all this time. And where there's Mother there's Father.

It never occurred to me that the one photo in a newspaper would be enough to bring him back into my life.

'Hello, Annie. You don't mind if I call you Annie, do you? How are you going? Very, very well by the look of you. Dad and me were just saying last night how much we missed you, wondering – all those years – where you were, how you were. You didn't even leave a note when you left.'

She opens her bag, takes out a large manila envelope and puts it on the table between us. 'Then, bingo! You turn up. Famous, sort of. Aren't you lucky we found you? I brought some lovely family photos to show you for old times' sake. We could get a lot of money for them from one of those internet sites. But maybe you'd like to buy them instead.'

Hanging On

'Nurrrrrse!' John Charles Sneddon shouts as loud as he can, which is not very loud. He listens for a response, the sound of feet coming along the corridor? Nothing.

His hands grope for the buzzer that is tangled among the bed sheets on his lap. He finds it, puts his thumb hard on the button and holds it there. Nobody comes.

He punches out his daughter's number on the mobile phone that is hanging around his neck. There's only the answering machine. 'Leave a brief message, I'll get back to you.'

'Ring me. There's nobody here to help me. I'm desperate,' he tells the machine.

She's never there. Work. That's all she thinks about. No time for him. Aileen will ring – when it's too late.

'Nuuuurse! Nuuuurse!' Mr Sneddon leans forward and listens. He can hear voices, he's sure of it.

'I have the right to live in my own bloody home, fall down my own bloody stairs, poison myself with my own bloody cooking and be incontinent in my own bloody bed,' he tells the empty room. 'But nobody takes any notice of me. And I'm not allowed to smoke. I'm not allowed to drink. I'm not allowed a visit to a women in her room. I told Aileen, and Geoff – that's her husband's name, isn't it, or is it Gerald? Whatever, I told them, over and over what they do to me. But will they listen? No.'

Mr Sneddon presses the buzzer again. The nurses don't understand what he says to them anyway and he doesn't understand them. They're from some other country. They have their own language.

All they can say is, 'Hello. Hello. Mr Sneddon. Howareyoutoday?'

'How am I? How do they think I am? I'm cooped up in here like a chook in a cage and they ask me how I am. How the hell do they think I am?' he says to no one and to everyone who's not there.

He knows why they don't answer the buzzer. They've got their feet up, having a cuppa tea. They don't care, none of them.

Mr Sneddon confides softly to the empty room, 'I didn't want to come here. I was all right in my own home. Aileen said I was starving. And that I couldn't look after myself. I know what that meant. It was a lie. I was clean. She's after the house. He's after the house. They can't wait till I'm gone.'

He phones his daughter again and leaves another message. Same words.

He tries to take his mind off what is happening by thinking about other things but he can't think of other things, only that he needs help.

'Nurse! Nurse!' he croaks. 'Nurse!'

Mabel is rolling past his door on her zimmer frame. She stops, turns and smiles then keeps walking. She goes round and round all day until she starts crying, then somebody takes her back to her room.

Mr Sneddon can hear a nurse somewhere down the other end of the hall. 'Nurse. Nurse! I need help!'

He is sure the nurse is the one with the bald head, a man. He's worse than the women. He bets on horses every day. That's all he worries about…or maybe it's that friend of Aileen's husband who does that.

Mr Sneddon is not sure whether lying still is best, or moving his legs is best. Lying still makes him think more about what is happening, but moving his legs makes it even worse.

He rings his daughter again, 'It's me. It's urgent. Urgent! I need you. Please, Aileen.' He doesn't know when she'll get back to him.

'Nurse! Nuuuuurse!'

Betty the ballerina dances by his door and he calls out to her. She thinks she's about to go on stage at Sadler's Wells, or the Bolshoi or the Sydney Opera House. Mr Sneddon knows the only place she ever performed was the Betty Smith School of Dance in Armidale.

'Betty! Betty! Where's the nurses?'

Betty pirouettes. For a wobbly moment, one foot rises a few centimetres from the ground. She smiles with red lips that match the red blobs on her cheeks.

Mr Sneddon shouts, 'Betty, have you seen a nurse?'

Betty curtsies then wafts off down the corridor still smiling. Who ever heard of a ballerina with the name Betty? She never stops smiling nor dancing. Even when she's in bed, she smiles. When Mr Sneddon was still able to move around the home he had seen her little short dress hanging on a chair in her room, which he was not allowed to enter.

Mr Sneddon clenches his teeth and squeezes his belly. It's agony.

'Somebody!' Mr Sneddon pleads.

With his forefinger, he carefully taps the buttons on the phone, drops it. It's in the bed somewhere ring-ring-ringing and he can't find it even with both hands, then it's beneath his legs under the sheet as well and he still can't find it. But he does and it's still voice of the 'I'll get back to you' woman, not Aileen live.

'NUUUURSE!'

None of them are going to help, neither nurses nor Aileen. But he suddenly knows who will help. Why didn't he think of them before. He taps out three short digits.

'You have dialled emergency triple zero. Your call is being connected,' a voice says.

Then, a proper woman, 'Do you need police, fire or ambulance?'

'I'm Charles Sneddon, I...'

'Do you need police, fire or ambulance?'

'I don't know, you see...'

'Do you need police? Fire? Or ambulance, sir?'

'I'm in the nursing home.'

'Which service do you require? Are you in danger?'

'How do I know which I need to...'

'That's all right. Take your time. I need to know which service you require: police or fire or ambulance?'

'There's nobody here to help me. Aileen won't ring me back.'

'What's your name please?'

'Charles. I …'

'Charles? Is that correct?'

'John Charles Sneddon, I've already told you, but I don't use my first name, John.'

'How old are you, Mr Sneddon?'

'Eighty-five, or was that the one before the last one? Eighty, eighty-eight. I had a party. In my own home.'

'What address are you at, Mr Sneddon?'

'Now?'

'Yes, now, today.'

'The nursing home.'

'Which nursing home?'

'This one.'

'Are you injured?'

'I, I, I need to…'

'Does that mean you are not injured?'

'No.'

'Then you are injured?'

'Of course not.'

'Are you in danger?'

'Yes.'

'Please, tell me your address, Mr Sneddon.'

'I've told you, the nursing home.'

'Which nursing home? Can you tell me exactly where it is please?'

'In town.'

'Do you know which town, Mr Sneddon?'

'I've forgotten but it will come back to me in a minute.'

'OK, take your time. But you are safe?'

'No! It's going to happen any minute.'

'What's going to happen?'

'Katoomba.'

'Is that the town you are in? But you don't know the name of the nursing home, is that correct? Is that correct, Mr Sneddon?'

Mr Sneddon knows he's just told her, but she doesn't listen. Nobody listens.

'Mr Sneddon, who do you think can help you best? The police? Ambulance? Fire service?'

'I'm not on fire, young woman. What's your name? It's not Aileen, is it?'

'My name's Evita.'

'Aileen won't speak to me. I've given up ringing her. I want to talk to the police.'

'I'm putting you through now.'

'Thank you. It took a long time.'

'This is the police. How can I help you?'

'I'm desperate. I need to go to the toilet. To pee. I'm busting and none of the nurses will help and Aileen's not talking to me.'

'The toilet? Are you taking the piss?'

'You're the police, you help people in trouble. My mother always said, go to the police if you're in trouble. I am in trouble. I'm at the nursing home. I can't hang on much longer.'

Takeaway

He steps out of the door into the cool and dark of the early summer morning and walks quickly down the road to the local park. There are not many people around this early, the best time of day, only a few runners and dog owners with pets that they treat like humans.

He jogs for a while, breathing deeply, taking life into his body, exhilarating in the freedom. He slows to a walk to prolong these moments in the open. In the few months he has been there, he has learned to recognise different birds from their calls as they waken in the first light and announce that they are ready for a new day. Each day is a day gained for him.

Long before the streets are busy with people on their way to work, he is back in his room, where he remains in self-imposed exile until evening. He will have spoken to only two people all day. One is the man from the house across the street who says good morning as he sets off on his walk. The man looks kind and he would like to get to know him, become friends even, but he dare not expose himself. You cannot tell from a person's looks how they will behave. He knows from experience. A kind man in Athens shared coffee with him at a little pavement café, then, mysteriously, police arrived. Luckily for him, he is quick to sense when things are about to change and he was on his feet and running as they jumped out of the police car. Yet he knows he must still trust people. What is life if you don't? You have lost. Those others have won.

Occasionally during the day, he sees his landlord, who rents him a room and use of a kitchen, but they never speak beyond basics. He would like to practise his English but conversations lead to personal questions. He feels people are probing, even if it is simply normal curiosity.

He watches the TV that is included in the rent he pays, but only the news channels, even though it is all bad, endless streams of people fleeing, from hell to hell. He watches for a chance glimpse of a familiar head. Important people keep saying the carnage and destruction must stop. But it doesn't. When he can no longer bear to watch, he lies on the single bed set against the window and looks out at the sky and the branches of a strange beautiful tree that grows in the small garden. Tiny cream flowers cloud the branches and the bark hangs in ragged sheets so fine he could write a letter on them. He can hear men and women passing in the street beyond the garden, and later in the morning children chattering their way to school. It makes him think of when he and his brother were little, kicking a ball made from a bundle of rags along the road to school, before the school and the rest of the town were destroyed.

Planes fly overhead moving their human cargo in and out of the country.

He has not heard from his brother for two weeks and he knows there are times when he will not have enough money to recharge his mobile phone account. He also knows how determined his brother is and will somehow find the cash and call, soon, but…who can tell? He dismisses the thought. He dozes restlessly as he readies himself for the night's work. He is troubled by bad dreams.

In the late afternoon, he leaves his room and walks quickly up the road, fifteen minutes to the restaurant where he works. Four men are squeezed into a small space which is the kitchen. They have learned to move around each other like dancers on a tiny stage without colliding as they prep food, cook, and wash the never ending pile of dirty pots in the clattering stainless steel sinks. In the occasional lulls, they go into the lane out the back of the restaurant for a breath of cool air. Even then, they do not share much of themselves; they have a reticence born of circumstances. Basic information is traded, names, usually false, little else. People do their work, take their money and go home, wherever home might be. They work there for a few weeks or a few months, then they are gone, no goodbyes, no farewell parties. Others take their place; they say hello, they smile, they nod. He has been there longer than anyone. He needs patience, time, luck. Despite his worries, he thinks he has all three.

The work peaks between seven p.m. and nine p.m., when the restaurant is usually full and takeaways are being whisked out on the backs of Uber Eats cyclists.

He had never heard of Thai cuisine until a few months ago; now it is his favourite food. When he finishes his shift at midnight, he goes home with a container full. During the evening, he will have sneaked leftovers from plates returned to the kitchen, even thought he knows he will lose his job if the manager sees him. It is another way of saving money.

After hours standing, the pain in his mangled back and legs is unbearable. It brings back memories he fights day and night to block out. He should seek treatment…maybe later when he has money to spare. But he must work where he can, when he can. Every night, cash is placed into his hand. The first thing he does when he gets back to his room is retrieve an envelope which is taped to the underside of a small cabinet next to his bed. Almost every dollar he has earned is in that envelope. He spreads the money flat on the bed and counts it, as he always does, before adding his earnings for the night. He puts a few dollars to one side, then counts the money from the envelope again.

He eases himself onto the bed, slowly stretches out and tries to sleep. He twists and turns and groans during the night, seeking a position of least pain. Soon he will have enough money for his brother.

He is anxious. He is always anxious, anxious about himself, anxious about his brother. Where he is. If he is.

*

His neighbour across the street, Matthew, is hungry. He tells his wife Ash, 'We should order the food now before the rush starts.'

She carries a couple of glasses of red wine into the garden and sets them down on the table. 'Pizzas?'

'Nah, I'm sick of pizzas, how about Thai?' Matthew takes a sip of wine.

'OK, you order. Try the Golden Triangle. They're always good,'

Matthew phones the Golden Triangle and a young woman with an Asian accent which is hard to understand answers. She finds him hard to understand too. Eventually, he hopes he has ordered what he wants: one serving of money bags, one of prawn rolls, one scallop pad cha, one eggplant wonder, and boiled rice.

'Half-hour. It will be delivered half-hour,' the girl repeats.

It can't come soon enough for Matthew, who has hardly had anything to eat since breakfast, unless you count a small salami sandwich in the middle of the day.

He goes back to the table, sits opposite Ash, stretches out his legs and has another sip of wine. He looks up at the grapevine that forms a canopy above his head and sights. 'This is the life, eh?'

'Could be a lot worse.'

He selects a fat, glistening black olive from a small bowl Ash has placed on the table and rolls it round in his mouth before carefully biting into it and allowing the sour juices to slide down his throat. He has another sip of wine. 'I don't feel like going back to work on Monday. I think I might extend the holiday into early retirement,' he jokes.

'There's a queue for that, and I'm at the head.'

'OK, maybe I'll put it off a bit longer. Someone has to keep paying taxes to buy French submarines,' Matthew says.

Ash sets up music and the soft strains of John Coltrane drift into the warm night.

Two glasses of wine later, Matthew complains that he is ravenous and wonders what the hell's happened to their dinner. He rings the Golden Triangle. Ater a few moments, he gets a recorded 'We can't come to the phone at the moment, leave a message and we'll get back to you shortly.'

'They must be flat out,' Ash says.

'They should employ more staff, then everybody would be happier: more jobs, better service, more tax for the government.'

'That'll be the day.'

'You wanta ring them again? You might have more success than me,' Matthew says after another ten minutes.

'What, some kind of intuitive feminist priority?' Ash says sarcastically.

'Just a thought. Wonder if it's burned down.'

'We'd have heard the fire engines. It'll be here any minute,' Ash assures him.

But the food doesn't arrive.

'I'm gonna go pick it up, they're bloody hopeless.' Matthew gets up and fumbles in his trouser pocket for his car keys.

''You're not driving, you're over the limit.'

'I'm not walking!'

'It'll do you good.'

'You go then.'

'Ah, just wait a bit longer,' Ash tells him.

Matthew sits down again, drinks. 'I'll give 'em five minutes.'

'Then?'

'I'll walk, you can come with me, keep me company.'

After five minutes, Matthew gets to his feet. 'Come on, let's go.'

'I'll stay and make up a dessert.'

'The walk will do you good.'

'No it won't.'

'OK. I'll be quick as I can.'

The hill seems steeper than normal. He shouldn't have had the last couple of glasses on an empty stomach. Walking makes him even hungrier. He passes the pizza shop and the smell of yeasty bread is almost enough to make him stop there, but he has already paid for the Thai food and he'll be there in twenty minutes, then twenty minutes back, so forty minutes – that's if it's ready– the hunter will return from the hills and they'll be eating.

He walks with the determination of a man whose mind is on his destination.

Almost there. He turns a corner, but the restaurant isn't where it should be, or if it is, it's invisible. He hasn't had so much to drink that he can't see it, surely. Then he realises the restaurant is there but there are no lights on, no tables outside. For the first time, he notices a crowd gathered on the footpath, heads turned towards the dark, silent building.

'What's going on?'

'We don't know,' a woman tells him.

Matthew squeezes his way through the group, cups his hands around his face and peers through big glass sliding doors into the dark interior. It is deserted. Tables still have plates of food on them, a dim light comes from the area of the kitchen at the rear. He knocks on the door. Shakes it but no one appears.

'We've been here half an hour,' a man's voice from behind says.

Matthew turns. Two couples stand forlornly clutching bottles of wine, reluctant to leave, hoping that if they stay long enough everything will be as it should be.

'I ordered takeaway hours ago and they never arrived. I've paid for it.' Matthew adds his complaint.

'We booked a table last month. It's my birthday. My mum's come all the way from the north coast, haven't you, Mum?' the woman says in exasperation, turning to a white-haired woman leaning on a zimmer frame who nods vigorously in agreement.

'It's a mystery, like the *Mary Celeste* – you know, the ship that was found adrift in the middle of the Atlantic with no one on board. A big table was set for dinner, but not a soul was there,' a woman's voice says from the crowd.

'Nothing was set for dinner, that's fiction,' her husband contradicts.

'It was. And no one ever found out what had happened to the crew,' his wife replies.

The combined irritation of the crowd is not enough to conjure activity from the Golden Triangle nor provide any answers. People begin to drift off muttering into the night. Matthew leaves the couple still arguing about the *Mary Celeste* and begins an irritated walk back home. He stops after a few hundred metres, leans against a wall, pulls out his mobile and rings the pizza parlour.

By the time he gets there, he only has five minute to wait before two hot, fragrant pizzas are slid into their boxes and he bears them down the street warm in his hands.

'What's that?' Ash's eyes open wide as Matthew strides into the garden and puts the pizzas on the table. He picks up his glass and takes a mouthful of wine.

'Pizzas.'

'What happened to the Thai?'

'It's gone.'

'How do you mean, gone? Restaurants don't go. Customers go, restaurants stay.'

'It's closed. Silent as the grave.'

He tells her what has happened as they sit at the table tugging their pizzas apart, and wondering.

*

Next morning, Matthew goes for his walk and picks up a newspaper from a shop on the main street. It's his one rebellion agains the digital age. He returns home and sits down at the table to eat breakfast, spreading out the paper and casually turning the pages. On page three there is a large photo of the Thai restaurant, under the headline 'Golden Triangle Illegals, police round-up in thieves kitchen.'

'Look at this!' Matthew calls out to Ash. 'No wonder they didn't deliver last night.'

He reads the story aloud, paraphrasing the contents to Ash. 'Seems everyone working in the kitchen was an illegal, and probably paid with the peanuts that didn't go into the satay sauce.'

Ash leans over his shoulder to look.

'The whole lot were carted off to an immigrant detention centre.' Matthew looks intently at the photo of police leading away the kitchen staff,. He points to one of the blurred heads, 'Look, that's the neighbour I see every morning. He worked there. Who'd have thought it, eh? An illegal living across the street.'

'Poor bugger,' Ash says.

'Yeah. Poor bugger. It was a good restaurant.'

The Flood

It was raining. Every day. All day. All night. It was never going to stop. In the bottom paddock, the three cows stood, heads down in soaked misery. Maggie felt sorry for them. She felt sorry for the chooks as well. And Greg the goat. And herself. And her mum and dad. And her younger brothers Bill and Jimmy, because it had been like that most of the month.

Rain thumped down on the bark roof of the house and found every crack and hole. The building creaked and flapped beneath the relentless wind. The track leading away from the farm towards town, twenty miles away, was all mud and puddles. Along the side of the house the rain-soaked ground was as gooey as her mum's porridge.

From the shelter of the veranda, Maggie couldn't even see the trees on the far ridge because of the grey curtains of water sweeping down the valley. The sand island of she-oaks in the middle of the river where she, Bill and Jimmy built gunyahs and lit campfires was almost underneath the surging brown torrent.

Maggie wondered whether she should bring the cows up to higher ground or wait till Mum and Dad came back with a wagonload of fence timber they'd been cutting. They said they'd be home early morning. It was now late afternoon. Maggie turned back into the house. Bill and Jimmy were wrestling on their bed in the corner of the one room.

'Stop! Yah promised Mum,' she yelled.

They ignored her until she grabbed Bill by the scruff of the neck.

'We was just playing,' Bill said indignantly.

'Well, yah can both play at feeding the chooks and Greg.'

'It's raining.'

'Don't tell me something I already know. Both ah yah. Go on.'

The boys unhooked two chaff bags from the back of the kitchen door, spread them over their heads and shoulders and stepped onto the veranda, then out into the rain. Maggie propped up the shutter and watched through the window as they splashed through the puddles at a run. The track was disappearing from sight in the growing gloom.

While the boys were busy at their chores, Maggie collected the pots and pans which were filling with water from the leaks in the roof. She flung the water into the yard then put the pots back in place. The ping and plop of water started again. It was driving her mad.

She swung a kettle off the fire where it had been simmering in readiness to make tea for their mum and dad and set it aside on the ashes.

Maggie took a loaf of cornbread from the tin and cut it into three thin slices. She brought in a hunk of pickled pork from the meat safe which hung under the veranda roof. She pared off three slices of pork.

The thump, thump of the boys running along the veranda announced their return. They burst into the kitchen dripping water, dried themselves on chaff bags hanging behind the door and sat down at the table with a bump.

'The chook shed's leaking, and half the roof's blown off,' Bill said.

'And there's nothing for 'em to eat,' Jimmy added in his squeaky voice.

'Mum and Dad'll be back soon,' Maggie said.

The boys picked up their cornbread and pickled pork and started to eat.

'You've been saying that all day,' Jimmy told her.

'They will be. Soon,' Maggie said with all the conviction she could muster as she pushed bread into her mouth.

'How soon?' Bill asked.

'How would I know? Soon means soon,' Maggie snapped.

The boys eyed each other over their slices of bread and kept eating.

'When you've finished yer teas, you'd better go to bed. There'll be lots to do tomorrow,' Maggie told them.

'We wanna stay up for Mum and Dad,' Jimmy said indignantly.

'They might'a decided to wait it out, give Big Boy a rest, they've got the wagon to shelter under, and a canvas. If they get back, they'll say goodnight. Promise.'

Bill and Jimmy finished their meal and dragged themselves reluctantly off to their bed.

Maggie cleaned up and put more wood onto the fire. It hissed like something living and the smoke buffeted back down the chimney.

'Bill!' she said after a while, 'Go ta sleep.' She had heard a rattling sound and knew that Bill was looking at his collection of bone spear heads that he'd picked up along the river.

Their dad had told him they was Black fella's stuff. 'If they stick one a them inta ya, yer dead,' he told the boys and ordered Bill to chuck them away.

But Bill hid them in an old tobacco tin, his secret. Except there were no secrets in this house.

Maggie pulled her mother's chair closer to the fire and sat watching the smoke. What if Mum and Dad hadn't camped overnight on high ground? What if they were somewhere down the track, soaking wet, Big Boy too exhausted to pull the wagon any further.

Maggie filled a lamp with kero and hung it outside under the veranda roof. They'd see it when they came over the ridge. She could hear the roar of the river below as it swept toward the sea. Then she sat again by the fire, listening to the incessant rain on the roof, and to the plop, plop of water.

What if Mum and Dad didn't come back tonight, or in the morning? What if they couldn't cross Two Mile Creek, or were bogged somewhere with a wagon load of fencing timber? What if they'd tried to cross a flooded Two Mile creek and…? Maggie tried to dismiss the idea.

What to do? Should Bill, Jimmy and her go to the high ground of the ridge above the track? But Mum and Dad had the canvas. They'd have nothing to shelter under. Should they try to walk out in the morning and meet up with Mum and Dad coming the other way? Should they stay put and hope for the best?

The questions went round and round in Maggie's head until she fell asleep. She had a nightmare in which she and the boys were lost in maze with water rising around them.

*

Maggie awoke to the grey light of another wet dawn, still in the chair by the side of a fireplace of white ash. She shivered and stretched her stiff neck. Bill and Jimmy were standing by her side, blankets draped over their shoulders.

'They didn't come,' said Bill, chewing his lip.

Maggie got out of the chair and did her best to smile. 'They'll be on the road again already. Get dressed. We'll do the chores early, a nice surprise for them.'

Maggie relit the fire and set the kettle near the back. She went to collect the pots under the leaks in the roof. Something wasn't right. The water in them wasn't parallel to the rim, the house was on a tilt that wasn't there yesterday evening. It was sliding in the waterlogged ground. Maggie stood with her hands on her hips and took three deep breaths. Then she went out to the veranda and dumped the water. She could just make out the cows in the paddock, huddled by the top fence. The river was halfway up their legs.

'Boys, quick! We've gotta bring the cows up. Now!'

Maggie knew she should have brought them up the day before. Unless they moved quickly, it would be too late. She grabbed her coat from behind the door, flung the chaff bags at the boys and plunged down the hill, skidding on the wet grass and mud, Bill and Jimmy trying to catch up, yelling, 'Wait for us! Wait for us.'

They waded through water that was up to Maggie's knees.

Maggie lifted the slip-rail and the animals plunged through, soft brown eyes wide with fear.

They urged them on till they reached the high paddock next to the house. The three of them stopped to regain their breath and turned to look at the river raging below. A clump of trees on the tip of their sand island bent under the force of wind and water. The trees tilted. They fell slowly and were swept away. Then one by one the remaining trees bent to the force of the water. And one by one each tree collapsed, to be washed away, a twisting, seething raft. In a moment, it was as though they had never been.

'We've gotta rescue Greg and the chooks,' Jimmy said, and set off at a run in the direction of a bark lean-to just above the house.

Maggie and Bill ran after him. Greg the goat was balanced on a pile of logs in a corner, stepping from one frightened hoof to another. The panicked chooks flapped and squawked on their perches above the water.

Maggie untied Greg and passed the rope to Jimmy, 'Hang onta him!' She flung open the door to the chook pen, 'They can look after themselves,' she said before Jimmy had chance to protest.

They struggled back to the house through driving rain. From the veranda, they looked up towards the barn. The track they had just run along had vanished beneath the water.

Jimmy knelt with his arms around Greg the goat, 'When are Mum and Dad gonna be here?' he said in a squeaky voice.

'Soon as they can.'

'We're all gonna drown,' he wailed.

'No, we're not. They'll be here soon even if they have to swim,' Maggie said.

'They can't swim,' Jimmy reminded her.

'Neither can you,' Bill said.

'I can, better 'n you.'

'Stop it!' Maggie yelled. 'Tie Greg in the corner. Mum'll go mad when she knows he's been in the house.

Jimmy didn't get a chance to tie up Greg before one of the walls began to cave in. Water poured through.

Maggie snatched the rope from Jimmy's hand, untied it, and slapped the goat on the rump, 'Go!'

'He'll drown,' Jimmy pleaded.

'He'll climb. Get yer chaff bags and a blanket, we're goin', 'Maggie yelled.

'My spears, I want…'

Maggie grabbed Jimmy's wrist. 'No!'

Bill took hold of the back of his pants.

'We're going up ta the ridge,' Maggie yelled.

She lifted the latch. The door burst in and water poured through, almost sweeping them off their feet.

Maggie looked around in desperation. 'Come on! Help me!'

She grabbed the kitchen table. The three dragged it out to the veranda and upturned it.

'Get on.' She pushed Jimmy and climbed on after him.

With one hand, Maggie gripped a veranda post. With the other, she held onto the table. Bill scrambled aboard. Maggie let go of the veranda post and Bill did the same. The table floated.

'What about…' Whatever Jimmy was going to ask was cut off.

'Hold tight. Real tight!' Maggie yelled.

The table bumped past the meat safe swinging above their heads. Past the window. Then off the end of the veranda into the swirling river.

Behind them, the house tilted, folded in on itself, then collapsed into the flood.

'Mum, Dad,' Jimmy wailed.

Maggie felt sick in the depth of her stomach but everything was happening so fast that there was no time to cry.

They were pulled in by the racing brown water with all the other debris scoured from the valley: uprooted trees, fences posts and rails, dead animals, haystacks and pig troughs. Twenty-five miles downriver was the sea.

The table twisted and turned in the eddies and flows of the speeding river, sometimes within yards of a green paddock or a wooded point, close enough to paddle the table to, if they'd had paddles. But not close enough to plunge into the water and struggle to the bank, particularly if you couldn't swim. Paddles! Why hadn't she thought of paddles?

Moments after almost touching land, they would be dragged out into the middle again, deep water below and all around. Bill and Jimmy were one minute full of excitement and hope as they swung close to land, then in dismay as they were pulled out to the middle once more. Bill wanted to make a rope from his belt and Jimmy's belt so he could splash his way to the bank next time they were close, but Maggie shook her head.

'Yah can only swim three strokes on a good day,' she told him.

He argued but he lost.

They swept past farmhouses with water up to their roofs. A house swept past them, a man, a woman clinging to the roof, a dog beside them. The people shouted, but they were too far and the water too fast and loud to able to understand.

Their table raft sped past passed Bomaderry, where the river had claimed the streets and the jetty, and boats drifted in vegie gardens.

Maggie knew they should have left the house earlier and gone to the ridge. Because of her, they were going to die.

The tiny craft reached the bar where river and sea met in a turbulent tumble of waters and windspray.

'Hang on, you two!' Maggie yelled.

Bill and Jimmy looked at her with terrified, pleading eyes.

Maggie wiped salt sea and salt tears from her cheeks. She had nothing left to offer but words. 'Hang on!'

'Mum! Dad!' Jimmy cried.

Bill roared at the top of his voice, as though sounds of his terror would save him.

They spun and bumped and were deluged with water as they were were driven relentlessly in the direction of the open sea. They cleared the submerged sandbars. And the chop and surge of the river gave way to the rolling, wind-blown waves of the Pacific Ocean.

*

The wagon rolled slowly down the incline. Darkness was closing in and what was left of the track was barely visible.

Sam walked in heavy boots beside a mud-spattered weary Big Boy, an encouraging hand on his flank. 'Nearly there, fella, nearly there.'

The newly split fence post and rails creaked in the back of the wagon as it lurched from side to side.

'I never thought we'd get across Two Mile Creek,' Lily said from her seat high on the wagon.

'I was worried for a minute – only a minute, though,' Sam called over his shoulder. He smiled to himself at the memory of crossing the creek. At the time, he thought he had misjudged the strength of the floodwater and they might lose everything, including their lives.

'I couldn't spent one more night in that rain,' Lily called down to him.

'You won't have ta,' Sam shouted as he guided Big Boy over a rough stretch. 'I can't see the house yet, can you?'

Lily relaxed her grip on the reins for a moment and stood. She shook her head and called back, 'Me neither.'

'They've not lit the lamps, saving kero.'

'I should still be able ta see it.'

'Yer tired.'

'Tired. Not blind, Sam.' Lily peered intently ahead. 'Sam! Sam. I…'

'I bet they'll be glad ta see us, eh.'

'Sam! It's gone! The house! It's gone! Where are they?' Lily screamed.

Sam pushed past Big Boy and ran sliding and falling down the track. Where the homestead should have been was a rectangle of sodden ground. Lily's chair and a chaff bag were caught in the low boughs of the tree that grew by the door, except that there was no longer a door. There was no longer a house.

Lily set off a wail that could have been heard throughout the valley if there had been someone one to hear. She clambered down from the wagon and collapsed on her knees.

Sam lifted her to her feet and held her upright. 'They'll a been rescued,' he said.

'Who by?' Lily clung to him, her fingers digging into his shoulders, her face hard on his chest. Her body shaking. 'Who was there ta rescue 'em? Tell me! Not us. We shouldna' left 'em. All for a few fence posts.'

'They'da got out well before the river was up 'ere,' Sam said as he rocked her back and forth. They'll be somewhere way up on the ridge sheltering under a rock or a hollow tree. Or somebody will 'ave…'

'Somebody! What Somebody? Everyone's washed away, or trying ta save themselves and their own.'

Sam helped Lily back onto the wagon, turned Big Boy around and drove to the high ground of the ridge, out of sight of where the house had been. He unharnessed Big Boy then hobbled him. In the short time left of daylight, they walked the ridge, the names of their three children ringing out among the trees as they called and called. No one answered.

When darkness was almost on them, Sam spread their canvas under the wagon. They crawled between the folds and lay on the cold hard ground clinging to each other. Sam tried to assure Lily that the children were safe, that they would have seen the danger coming and got out. His persistence gave her hope. They planned where they would search the following day and they waited throughout the long sleepless night for daylight. They could hear Big Boy snorting and pawing the ground hungrily.

When the sun rose over the horizon into a brilliant blue sky, Sam and Lily resumed their search. They began on the high ground where the three children could have found refuge among whatever trees had not been cleared. They checked fallen hollowed out old gums where they might have sought shelter. They called and cooeed along the ridges but no one called back.

The only life they found was some of their hens, roosting in a tree. Sam caught one. He insisted that they rest and have food. On a smoky fire, Lily mechanically prepared a soup. Her earlier hope had turned again to despair and she sat curled in on herself, looking blankly at the fire.

Sam coaxed her into eating. 'You've gotta keep yer strength up, for them. Get that inta ya. Then we'll go downstream. They mighta got up a tree, or…' His voice tailed off.

Lily shook her head without looking at him.

They left the ridge and began to work along the bank of the receding river. They both knew the worst thing they were looking for but they did not give it words.

The carcasses of dead cattle and the occasional horse were wedged in trees. Others lay among the edge of the water. Crows flapped off, cawing as they approached. They perched in trees and waited for them to pass so they could return to their scavenging. Throughout the day, Sam and Lily trod the land between the high water mark and the riverbank as they searched for footprints or any indication that the children had been there.

They clambered over uprooted trees and skirted entanglements; they looked with dread for a familiar piece of clothing…or something they didn't want to imagine. They came across remnants of life from farms further up the valley, a cart, a tin bathtub, a drawer from a chest, shoes and other articles of clothing. The sight reminded them how far things could float and, if human, could possibly survive.

They came across no other person on their side of the river, nor did they see anyone on the other side. With the sun setting, they returned to the wagon and spent another sleepless night on hard ground in whispering comfort. They prayed.

Next morning, Sam threw the fencing timbers off the wagon. The search of the riverbank was over. There were other places the children might have escaped to. He harnessed Big Boy and they left their land and set off for Bomaderry.

The track was washed out in many places. Sam and Lily dragged rocks to fill in gullies that had been scoured in the road. They hacked and pulled, and with the help of Big Boy, dragged fallen trees aside. Progress was slow.

Yet another sleepless and comfortless night was spent beneath the wagon. The usual one-day trip took two back-breaking days. They saw not another person or animal. The valley was swept clear of everyone and everything.

Riding into Bomaderry was like entering a town that had been vanquished by an invading army. The streets were almost deserted. Scarcely a house remained standing; others were just foundations. Everything within reach of the hungry waters bore its marks. Boughs, and sometimes whole trees, were strewn everywhere. The contents of homes lay in the stinking mud that covered everything the waters had touched: someone's bed frame, a woman's battered hat, a boot, a rocking chair, a dead dog, a piano.

Sam and Lily begged information from anyone they passed, 'Have you seen our Maggie, and Bill, and Jimmy?'

They were met with sad shaking heads, faces that were comatose with shock. The general store a little way up the hill from the river, a converging point for those going into town, was locked and shuttered. The only place open was the new bank higher up the hill. They tethered Big Boy to a rail outside and followed a muddy trail into the bank. They asked the teller the same question they had asked every other person they met.

They received the same answer and shake of head. 'Really sorry, Mr and Mrs Johnston. Really sorry. Not heard a word.'

Sam and Lily climbed back onto the wagon and started down the hill. They turned into any place that had once been a street, calling three names into the emptiness in the hope that by some miracle the children would emerge from a house that had been spared, or from the ruins of another.

A hollowness grew in their bellies with each hour. It became obvious even to them that the three were not there.

Finally, they halted the wagon once more. Sam sat, his head bowed, the reins limp in his hands. Lily could look at nothing.

Eventually Sam turned to her. 'They're gone, lass. We'll never see 'em again this side a heaven. Everyone in the district knows our three. If they'd been rescued, everyone'd be talking about it.' He put his arm across Lily's shoulders and drew her thin, shaking body into him.

They sat in silence for a long time.

'Let's get back then,' Sam eventually said.

Lily shook her head vehemently. 'Never. Never am ah gonna go back there. Never. Never. Never. I wanta go home.'

'That's home.'

'No. Could ya wake up every morning for the rest a yer life and look down that valley at the river? We settled there because of that river, an' it took away everything we live for. We can't go back there. Take me home, Sam.'

'Ireland?'

'Where else?'

Sam sat for a long time in silence. Then he wheeled Big Boy around and the weary horse pulled the wagon through the drying mud and up the hill. Sam stopped outside the bank as a man was leaving, a ticket-of-leave convict who they knew only as Wilson. He too had twenty acres further up the valley. Sam called out to him, then jumped down from the wagon and went over.

Lily watched as they talked. After some time, they came back to the wagon together.

'Here's the new owner of Big Boy and the cart,' Sam said to Lily.

'I'll take ya wherever ya need ta go,' Wilson said.

Lily sat for a moment, then climbed down. She put her arms around Big Boy then kissed him on the soft nose.

Sam patted the horse on the side of the face. 'G'bye, Big Boy. Look after him,' he said to the new owner.

'Ah will,' Wilson replied.

*

The first steamer to tie up at the wharf since the flood was manoeuvring into position when Sam and Lily came away from the bank. They had the small amount of cash they had saved over the years, plus the money from the sale of Big Boy and the wagon. They crossed the empty wharf and boarded the steamer for Sydney.

They spoke to no one on the almost empty vessel as it hugged the coast and sailed north on an ocean that was as brown as a ploughed paddock. They walked the deck, arms linked, each in their own silent darkness. Sam's earlier optimism had given way to despair when they failed to find any sign of the children in Bomaderry. Words of comfort and hope they had found for each other when they had begun their search were no longer there.

On reaching Sydney, Sam and Lily went from the steamer straight to a shipping office on the wharf. The talk among the crowd inside was all about the disaster. Everyone was hungry for information, or anxious to tell a story.

'Do ya know anybody in the floods?' a grizzled man asked them as they waited to buy tickets.

Sam and Lily shook their heads.

'I've gorra son and his wife there. They gor out. Lost everything, though. I'd warned…'

Sam and Lily turned away. The man found another ready audience. Sam and Lily stayed close to each other and tried to block their ears.

They booked two berths on the next steamer to England and fled the ticket office.

They bought what items they needed for the voyage, then found lodgings in The Rocks, close to the wharves. They hid with the weight of grief behind the blinds of their room.

'What was we thinking, leaving 'em in that weather?' Lily said over and over.

Sam tried to find words to console her but was crushed with guilt. 'It was me insisted. If I'd…' Sam couldn't get the thought out of his head.

They waited for the day of sailing, going out only to eat each night.

*

The table raft spun and bobbed on the flood peak of the swollen river, where it spewed into a sea, silt-brown as far as the blurred horizon.

'We'll be washed up along the beach somewhere,' Maggie shouted, as she tried to console her brothers, who were clinging to the sides of the table, too frightened to raise their heads as they were swept out to sea and descending darkness.

Maggie again silently cursed her own stupidity. If they'd had any bits of wood, they'd have paddled the table ashore on an eddy of the river. It would have been so simple.

She looked back towards land. So close. So far, and getting further. She wiped water from her stinging eyes and choked back sobs. North of the river's mouth she could make out a line of breakers, and on the beach…a faint glimmer of light, a fire? People?

She screamed, 'Help! Help pleas help us!' over and over and waved frantically, knowing no one could see, nor hear.

The boys looked up at her, blank-faced.

The light of the fire disappeared behind the waves, then reappeared. Then was gone again.

'Ya all right, Jimmy? Bill? I'll work something out,' Maggie called.

She strained her eyes towards the shoreline. She could no longer see the beach. But the light kept reappearing. It even seemed closer. It was not possible. But there it was again. Then gone. It wasn't on the beach, it was on the ocean, and moving towards them.

Bill yelled, 'Look!'

Jimmy turned, 'What?'

'A light.'

'Ah saw it too!' Maggie said.

'Liars!' Jimmy screamed.

'It is. I…'

Before Maggie could finish, Bill yelled again, 'Yeh! Yeah! There!' He pointed.

There was only grey ocean.

Then the pale light appeared, and was gone.

'I know wha… It's on a boat,' Maggie shrieked.

'There's a man rowing,' Bill shouted. 'He goes inta a trough, then comes up agin. There's a lamp.'

'Is he gonna rescue us?' Jimmy whispered in a voice only he heard.

'Paddle!' Maggie yelled, and they all splashed and paddled with their hands in a futile effort to move the table towards the boat.

'It's a Black! A Black fella!' Maggie said in disbelief as the figure turned towards them.

'He'll spear us,' Jimmy whimpered.

'Shurrup,' Bill ordered.

A dozen more strokes and the Black was level. He shipped the oars and grabbed the side of the table with one hand. 'Hold on!'

Bill and Maggie reached out and grasped the bobbing boat.

'Yah ready?' he asked in a gravelly voice. 'One at a time, the little'n first.'

Maggie and Bill gripped the boat with all their strength. Jimmy crawled to the edge of the table. He wobbled.

The Black grabbed him by the shoulders and heaved him into the stern. 'Stay there!' He leaned out to Bill. 'Get on all fours.' Gripping him under the arms, he swung Bill into the bow as boat and table almost swung apart. 'Don't let go yer table!' he yelled.

Boat and table rocked and thumped into each other, then swung apart. Maggie tried to hold them as she shuffled into the centre to keep the balance.

The Black stretched out a hand. 'Now, missy. Step over. Don't be scared.'

Maggie reached towards the hand, she hesitated, then grabbed.

The Black swung her into the pitching boat. He turned to Bill, 'Now!'

He let go of the table. Bill did the same. In a moment, the table was gone. Their rescuer dug his oars into the water, spun the boat around and began rowing towards an invisible shore.

Occasionally, he offered words of encouragement to the three children, crouched cold and shivering in the bottom of the rolling boat. Mainly he was silent except for loud, rhythmic grunts of exertion. Slowly, they crept closer to land until they could see a vague line of white surf gnawing at the beach.

A full moon had risen behind them, white on the sea. The Black steered the rowboat north of the turbulent river mouth to where water flowed shallow over submerged sandbanks. To the south, stretched a long surf beach.

Eventually, he beached the boat and jumped ashore. He reached out, grasped Jimmy under the arms.

'No! I'll…' Jimmy protested feebly as he was swung out of the boat and onto the sand, where he sank to his knees.

Bill got unsteadily to his feet and made his way to the bow. The Black lifted him clear and set him down next to his brother.

Finally, he reached out. Maggie grabbed his arms and was swung clear. She leaned on the Black as he helped her a few yards up the sand, where she collapsed.

The Black dragged the boat above the high water mark and untied the lamp from the bow. 'Can ya walk?' he asked them.

'Yyyes,' Maggie said through chattering teeth.

She and Bill struggled to their feet and took a few steps. Bill pulled Jimmy upright. His young brother stood. Unsteadily.

The Black stepped forward and swung Jimmy onto his back, then, holding the lamp high, he set off into the darkness.

'I'm not'a baby,' Jimmy protested feebly.

After a few hundred yards, they entered a clearing where a large gunyah had been built against a sprawling banksia tree. The Black disappeared inside with Jimmy. Maggie stopped.

Bill pushed her. 'Go on.'

Maggie stooped and went in. The dim light of the lamp revealed a tucker box sitting on sandy ground that was covered with paperbark and strewn with possum skins and blankets.

'Get yer clothes off,' the Black said.

Maggie, Bill and Jimmy huddled together shivering.

'Go on. Yah'll get sick. Get 'em off." The Black threw blankets at them. 'Get them wet things off!' He turned his back and began to kindle a fire in the entrance.

Bill was first to strip off, shirt and pants. He wrapped a blanket around himself then tugged the clothes off a resistant Jimmy. Maggie turned her back. She cloaked herself in a blanket, and wrestled with her clinging, soaked dress, then her pantalettes. She dropped them at her feet and pulled the blanket tighter.

The Black indicated the ground near the fire. 'Sit there. Ah'll boil the billy.'

'Do ya know…' Maggie began to ask.

'Later,' the Black said.

The three sat, wrapped in their blankets, Jimmy wedged tightly in the middle, mouth open with fatigue and fear.

By the time the Black had a billy of tea ready, the three lay oblivious to the world.

*

When Maggie awoke, the sun was blinking through the leaves of banksia trees outside the gunyah. She thought for a moment that she was on the farm, with sun shining through the shutters. She sat up. This wasn't the farm. This was…? She remembered; the river; the sea, the terror, the Black lifting them into his boat, then this place.

She looked around. Bill and Jimmy were like two sleeping seals under their blankets. She could hear them breathing softly. A wisp of smoke drifted from the remains of a fire, a frying pan and the billy beside it. There was no sign of the Black. Maggie wanted to get up and out of the gunyah but she could not keep her eyes open. She pulled the blanket over her head for a few more minutes rest.

When she woke again, it was dark. She could smell food. The Black was sitting next to the fire, his back to her. The boys were still curled up asleep.

The Black asked without turning round, 'Yah hungry?'

Maggie nodded. 'Yeah. What ya gonna do with us? We want our mum 'n' dad.'

'Ya need tucker 'n' rest.'

'Where are they?'

The Black shrugged.

'Do ya know?'

'Everything's a mess-up wi' the floods.'

Maggie pulled the blanket tighter. She looked for her clothes, they were where she had dropped them, wet, and covered in sand.

She sat, staring at the Black. 'What's yer name?' she asked hesitantly, 'I'm Maggie Johnston and…'

'I know who ya are.'

'What's yer name?' Maggie asked again.

'Albert.'

'Our farm's…'

'And I know where yer farm is. It was given ta ya. I know it real well.'

Maggie was afraid to say more.

'Sit near the fire,' he told her.

She hesitated.

'I've had breakfast. I'm not gonna eat ya.'

Maggie got to her feet. She wrapped her blanket tightly around herself, then walked towards the fire on wobbly legs. She lowered herself to the ground and hugged her knees. Albert handed her a tin plate with a large fish on it.

'What yah gonna do with us?'

'Eat that first.'

Maggie took the plate and pulled the fish apart, cramming the pieces into her mouth.

Albert poured tea, black as the billy it came from. Maggie picked up the pannikin and drank. The scalding, sweet tea flowed warm into her belly.

When she had finished eating, she again asked the Black when they were going to find their mum and dad.

'Whenever we can.'

Their voices woke the boys.

Jimmy rubbed his eyes and looked around in bewilderment, then fear. 'Maggie! What…?'

'Yer all right. Do yah remember what happened?' Maggie asked.

Jimmy sat in silence, then nodded.

Bill sat up, he stared at Albert then looked at Maggie with expectant eyes.

'Ya all right?' Maggie asked.

Bill shivered and pulled his blanket tight. He nodded.

'Sit here,' Albert said and moved aside to give them space closer to the fire.

The boys stepped cautiously forward and sat down. He handed them hunks of fish and a pannikin of tea.'

'Ya'll have to share the tea,' he said.

They grabbed the food and stuffed it into their mouths.

'Where are we?' Bill, looked up and asked between chewing.

'Same place as ya was when I pulled ya outa the water,' Albert said.

'Do ya know what happened ta our mum 'n' dad?' Jimmy asked.

'Eat up. You'll need yer energy. Then get back ta sleep.' Albert lay on his side near the fire and closed this eyes.

Maggie hung their damp clothes from the roof of the gunyah and the three huddled close under their blankets at the edge of the firelight.

'What's he gonna do with us?' Jimmy whispered.

'We'll be OK,' Maggie told him. 'We'll find Mum 'n' Dad.'

They sat and waited, the only sounds the crashing of the sea on the beach and the wind roaring in the trees. Each of the three silently re-lived the terror of the past days, and felt a growing fear for their future. Eventually, one by one, they succumbed to exhaustion, Maggie was the last to fall asleep.

*

They were woken in the morning by the roar of wind in the trees and the sound of surf pounding the beach. The rain had stopped but the wind had increased in strength. They pulled on their clothes and stepped out of the gunyah. There was no sign of Albert, but a wisp of smoke drifted from a smouldering log on the fire.

'We can ger away before he comes back,' Jimmy whispered.

'Maybe he's not coming back,' Maggie said.

'He wouldn't rescue us 'n' leave us t' die,' Bill reasoned.

'Please,' Jimmy's squeaky voice pleaded, 'let's go.'

He pulled Maggie by the arm onto a faint path. It took them past a shallow lagoon to the beach. Albert's boat was pulled up on the sand. The tide was high and the surf big. South were sandbars and the mouth of the dark, fast-moving river. North, as far as they could see, were breakers and windswept beach strewn with whole trees that had been washed down river by the flood and brought back in on the tide, stripped of their leaves and small branches. Inland was dense bush.

Jimmy tugged at the boat. 'Let's take it. I can row.'

'Through the surf? Up the river?' Bill sneered. 'You're a bloody goose, Jimmy.'

'We'll walk then,' Jimmy replied defiantly.

'Where to?' Bill asked.

'Town.'

'There ain't no town no more,' Bill yelled. 'Did ya see one?'

They made their way back to the camp. A rusty tin half full of flour was sitting just inside the gunyah. They built up a smoky fire. Maggie mixed the flour with water and when the fire had burned down to coals she made damper. It stilled the gnawing emptiness of their stomachs.

'The flour won't last long. What if he doesn't come back?' Maggie said.

'We'd starve,' Jimmy added.

Bill chewed his lip. He sighed, 'Damn! Come on then.'

'Where?' Jimmy asked.

'Where ya said. Town! What's left of it,' Bill snapped. 'If we can find it.'

They each draped a blanket over their shoulders and walked out of the camp.

They quickly met their first obstacle, a tangle of trees recently brought down. They went around them, scrambled through dense, head-high wattle that grabbed their legs and sent them sprawling. They gained a few hundred yards and came across more downed trees and wattle thickets. The pattern was repeated until, hot and scratched, they faced the fact that they'd never get out trying to crash through trackless bush.

They returned disconsolately to the camp and flopped down inside the gunyah. There was still no sign of Albert. All they could do was wait, and hope he returned.

Late in the afternoon, he emerged silently from the bush. 'Somebody's gonna come for yah,' he said as they stood hopefully in front of him.

'Dad?' Maggie asked, a smile of relief beginning in the corner of her mouth.

'Somebody,' Albert said impatiently.

'When?' Bill asked suspiciously.

'Tomorra. Day afta. Day afta that. When they can get 'ere.'

'Will they know where Mum and Dad are?' Maggie asked.

'You'll have ta ask them.'

'Where they gonna take us?' Bill asked.

'Outa 'ere.'

They stayed in the camp all the following day, waiting, hopeful. No one arrived.

In the early afternoon of the second day, a white man with a long beard emerged from the bush riding a big grey horse. He reined in and climbed slowly down, adjusting a musket slung across his back. 'Ya ready?'

'Where we goin'?' Maggie asked nervously.

'Somewhere clean and dry. Come on, it's a long way.'

'Where's our mum 'n' dad?' Maggie asked hopefully.

'Don't know.'

One by one, he gave each a leg-up onto the back of the grey; Maggie was in the saddle, holding the pommel, Jimmy sat in front of her, gripping a fistful of mane, Bill was at the back, his arms wrapped around Maggie.

The horseman turned the grey in the direction of the narrow track he had come down. He stopped. For a moment, he looked back, Albert was standing in the clearing, watching, waiting for him to say something.

The horseman nodded, almost imperceptibly. 'Thanks.' Then he set off, leading the grey by the bridle.

Maggie looked back, 'Thanks, Albert, fer rescuing us!'

'Yer, Albert,' Bill added. 'Thanks. Thanks!'

Jimmy kept his gaze fixed on the horses ears and the bush ahead.

Albert raised one hand slightly. A moment later, he was lost from view.

The four travelled all day and into the night with barely a stop. Sometimes, they made detours around masses of tangled, windblown trees, other times they traversed the banks of swollen creeks until they found a safe place to cross.

If the going was easy and the track clear of fallen branches and downed trees, the three sat, swaying high on the back of the grey. When it was rough, they walked, putting one weary foot before the other, longing for journey's end.

Their rescuer told them his name was George. His horse was Snowball. Other than that, he spoke little. His brow was furrowed, as though he was lost in his own troubled thoughts. His mouth, what they could see of it under his beard, was clamped tight.

The few words he did utter created a bleak picture. He told them, with a shake of his head, that there was little left of the town and little left of the people. They pleaded with him to tell more, but he shook his head.

*

When Snowball finally plodded along the waterlogged rutted remains of the road into Bomaderry, the children looked out over a ghostly mud-covered moonscape. Almost nothing of the town remained except the occasional remnants of a house. George led the horse to one of the few intact buildings, the general store. A faint light glowed from the windows.

'This is it,' he said, tying Snowball to the veranda post. 'Mr and Mrs Walsh'll look after ya as good as yer own mum 'n' dad would.'

He reached up, and one by one lifted the exhausted children down from the horse. They huddled together, too tired and too bewildered to move. The door of the store burst open.

'Oh! At last, you're here.' A tall, thin woman stood wringing her hands before running into the street and trying to embrace all three children at once. 'We thought you were gonners.'

'Where's Mum and Dad?' Bill asked in a plaintive voice.

'They're safe. Come on, we'll talk about it later. Ya must be starving.'

'Where are they?' Maggie pleaded.

A small, rotund man stepped out of the door into the street. He stood next to his wife and shook his head slowly from side to side. 'I don't believe it, safe. God bless Albert,' he said to no one in particular.

'Put Snowball in the stable, then come in for a bite to eat,' Mrs Walsh called to George.

George shook his head and led Snowball away.

'They're not here, but they are all right. I've had soup on the stove all day,' Mrs Walsh said, turning back to the children. 'We didn't know when you were gonna get here.'

She and Mr Walsh guided the weary children into a store which smelled of stagnant water. Every box and basket had been lifted clear of the floor and stacked on shelves and a long counter, away from the floodwater.

'We've only been open a few days,' she told them. 'The mess. The mess! But we saved most things. Not that there's many people to sell to.'

She herded the children behind the counter and ushered them up a flight of wooden stairs into a kitchen. 'Sit there,' she indicated a table, and they flopped down onto a bench, barely awake.

'We'll get something inside you.' She ladled out three bowls of soup which were immediately demolished.

'Now, come with me.'

Lamp in hand, she and Mr Walsh guided the teetering children into a nearby room which contained a large bed.

'Get into that. Don't worry about your clothes.' Mrs Walsh spread extra blankets over them and stood looking lovingly down.

'What about…' Jimmy's voice squeaked from the bed.

'Mum and Dad? In the morning when you've had a good night's sleep.'

Towing their shadows behind them in the pale light of the lamp, Mr Walsh and Mrs Walsh retreated across the room to the door.

'Please.' It was Jimmy again. 'Can you leave the lamp?'

When the door was closed behind them, Mrs Walsh leaned her head on her husband's chest and cried with relief. 'What a mess. What a mess.' She eased herself away and looked up at her husband. 'But one woman's curse is another woman's blessing.'

'How we going to tell them?' he asked.

*

It was almost noon the following day before Maggie, Bill and Jimmy woke. Mr and Mrs Walsh sat them down in the kitchen, each with a bowl of porridge. It was time to answer their question.

'When your mum and dad got back to the farm and it was all gone, they searched everywhere. They asked everybody. Not a soul in the valley nor in town here had seen hide nor hair of you since that great wall of water had come rushing through. They were sure you was all drowned.'

'But where are they?' Jimmy demanded.

After a long silence, Mrs Walsh answered, 'They've gone back to England, or Ireland.'

'They've left us!' Jimmy wailed.

'They didn't know ya was alive.' Mr Walsh reached out for Jimmy's hand but Jimmy snatched it away.

He dropped his arms onto the table and hurried his head. His body shook with silent sobs.

Mr Walsh sighed. Eventually, he said. 'Nobody knew, Jimmy. People drowned. George lost his wife.'

'What we gonna do?' Maggie began to weep.

'They coulda stayed. Looked harder,' Bill cried. 'We'll never see 'em again.' He fought to hold back tears, and failed.

'We'll take care of the three of you,' Mrs Walsh said, wiping her eyes with the back of her hand.

Jimmy's tear-bloated face emerged from his arms, 'I don't want you, I want Mum and Dad.

Mrs Walsh reached out and held him gently by the shoulders. 'You'll be like one of our own.'

'Everything ya need,' Mr Walsh added.

'Find 'em! Pleeese, find 'em,' Maggie cried.

*

The SS *Tilbury* towered above Sam and Lily as they shuffled up the crowded gangplank on the Sydney wharf. They had little to carry on board and nothing in the hold. Soon they would be on deck watching Australia disappear behind them.

Only a short time before, Sam and Lily had had three bonny, healthy children, a block of land and a home. Now all they had was each other. Sam had gone from convict, to free man, then a tenant farmer of twenty acres. One day through his industry, he would have owned his own farm and Lily would have been a farmer's wife, not a maid again.

But the one-room slab and bark homestead that Sam had built was gone. The small farm buildings he and Lily had put up together were gone. So was the stock they had slowly acquired through haggling and borrowing. The paddocks they had hacked out of the bush were buried under debris, uprooted trees and river sand.

Sam and Lily found a corner on deck out of the sun and away from the chatter of the other passengers. They sat silently, side by side. Lily reached out and took Sam's hand. He did not look up.

'Sam. Sam,' she said softly.

Eventually, he turned. The face of an old man looked at her. Lily placed her hand on his neck and kept it there.

After a while, the voices of other passengers penetrated Lily's mind. She became aware of one repeated word, 'miracle'.

Eventually, curious, she got to her feet and asked a women and her husband who were close by with two little boys what was all the talk of a miracle.

'Haven't ya heard?' the woman said in disbelief. 'Three kids, one girl, two boys, was found floating on a lump of wood on the south coast during the floods. Parents was drowned. It were a miracle they was saved.'

'Some fella in a fishing boat got 'em, and it weren't a lump a wood they was on, I heard it were a table. Can you believe it? They was washed out past the bar of the Shoalhaven River afore they was picked up,' her husband said.

'Nearly dead, poor little things. If that's not a miracle, nothing is. Gives you faith, it does,' his wife added.

'The parents was drowned,' her husband repeated. 'Musta put the kids on the table, sacrificed themselves.'

'Where are they, the children?' Lily cried, grasping the woman's sleeve.

'With them as runs the general store at Bomaderry, so ah heard,' the woman said, pulling free.

Lily turned to Sam. 'Did yah hear that?'

Sam looked up.

'It's gotta be be them,' Lily said, struggling to speak. She repeated what she had heard.

Sam pulled himself to his feet. For the first time in weeks, Lily saw a flash of the Sam she had married.

'Who told ya all this?' he demanded.

'Everybody down there knows. They're all talkin about it,' the man said.

'Did you see the kids?'

'I didn't have ta. Don't believe me if ya don't want, mister,' said the woman

'I do want. I do. Maybe we gave up too soon,' Sam said, grabbing Lily by the arm.

He forced his way through the crowd on deck, then down the gangplank against protesting embarking passengers.

Lily hung on behind, clutching his shirt, sobbing with excitement, shouting, 'It has to be them, Sam. It has to be!'

They ran along the crowded wharf, dodging and weaving, thrusting aside those who did not get out of the way quickly enough. They barged to the front of the queue in the shipping office and pleaded with the clerk until he agreed to cancel their tickets to England. They booked passages on a coastal steamer heading south the next day.

When morning came after a sleepless night swinging between hope and disbelief, they left their lodgings. A few hours later, they were aboard the steamer *Southern Cross*, rolling through the Heads then butting its way south.

'What if it's not them?' Sam said yet again, as they wove their way between passengers on the crammed deck.

'It has to be. How else could there be two boys and a girl found like that? A coincidence couldn't happen,' Lily said.

'Until we see 'em, we won't know. It could just be...' Sam tailed off. He was sure she was right, but, but what if...?

Most of the night they paced the deck, side by side, oblivious of the chill tail wind that pushed the *Southern Cross* down the coast. Earlier, Lily had quizzed everyone who would listen if they knew of the miracle. Some said three girls had been rescued way out at sea. Someone else had heard it was dolphins that carried them into the shallows. Yet others told them that one child, they weren't sure whether boy or girl, had been washed up half dead on a beach north of the Shoalhaven. Their brother and sister had been drowned. All agreed on one thing: a child, or children, had, one way or another, been saved from the flood.

Sam and Lily asked themselves the same questions over and over: why hadn't they searched for Maggie, Bill and Jimmy for longer? Why had they given up? If it was Maggie, Bill and Jimmy, or even one of them, what would they think of their parents for leaving them? What if if wasn't them but some other unfortunate orphans?

Sam and Lily were still on deck when the first light of day touched the sea in the east and the moon sank behind the emerging coastline to the west. They held each other and silently prayed that their children were alive.

For another day and night, they paced and fretted and curled up together without sleeping.

*

Finally, Bomaderry wharf sat square and solid in the morning sunlight. The Shoalhaven River, which had been a raging brown torrent, now sparkled in the sunlight as it flowed obediently between its banks. Nests of flood debris hung in trees high up the river bank. Despite a breeze, the smell of dampness and decay hung in the air.

Sam and Lily were first down the gangplank when it was lowered with a thump onto the wharf. Despite having barely slept for days, they almost ran towards the general store.

They opened the door to the all-pervading smell of the river. A dark flood stain marked the bottom of the walls and along the front of the long counter.

Mr Walsh turned from where he was stacking shelves. 'Can I help y… Mr and Mrs Johnston! We thought you'd sailed for England…' He got no further.

'Mum! Dad!'

A figure hurled across the store. Maggie. She flung herself at her parents. Seconds later, Bill and Jimmy appeared – they stopped, and stared.

'You left us,' Jimmy finally said in a whisper.

'Yer like three ghosts, 'cept yer alive. I need ta touch ya to make sure.' Their father stepped towards them, arms extended.

Bill leaped on him, almost knocking him to the ground.

Jimmy stood, choking back sobs. 'Why did ya go?'

'We was told that you was on a ship. But yer still here,' Maggie said as she clung, first to Sam, then to Lily, then back again to Sam.

Their father gathered Jimmy and Billy in and they hung on to each other.

*

That night, they all crammed round the Walsh kitchen table and swapped their stories. Sam and Lily announced that they would return to the block and start again. No river was going to drive them off their land. They'd build another slab and bark house, all of them, together. They'd buy more chooks. Perhaps a couple of pigs. They'd put up new fences. They'd buy cows. Maybe Gregory the goat had swum to safety and was waiting for them, Sam said.

'Back in the Old Country I'd be nothing but farm labourer, and Lily, a maid. Here, we'll have our own place. The boys'll make good farmers,' he said to Mr and Mrs Walsh.

'And ya've gotta buy back Big Boy,' Jimmy told him.

The children scrambled to tell their parents how they were swept away, how they fought the river, how they thought they were never going to see their parents again until they were all in heaven; and how they were rescued, by a Black called Albert.

'And they finished up here with us safe and sound,' Mrs Walsh said, trying hard to smile and hide her disappointment. 'They'll always be welcome in this house. Always.' She sniffed and choked back the lump in her throat.

Mr Walsh reached under the table for her hand and held it tight.

'Who was he, that Black, Albert?' Sam asked.

'He comes into town once in while. But he doesn't hang around like some of 'em. His mob lived along the river and up into the ridges where your block is. He knows the coast like the back of his hand, every sandbar, every rip, every river mouth. The kids was real lucky it was him that spied them,' Mr Walsh added.

'I can't believe he did what he did. So brave. He coulda drowned. We gotta repay him somehow. How can we?' Lily asked.

'You can't.' Mrs Walsh shook her head. 'You can't.'

A Good Crop

Isobel watches him walking down the road towards her. Her heart jumps. His name is Nick and she has known him for two months. He is so handsome. The way he walks, head high, lean muscular body and long legs that carry him fluid as water down the road, his head turning side to side as though he is afraid of missing something. He smiles at all the girls and they smile back.

Nick sees her, he waves. He grins, he runs across the road dodging the traffic and envelopes her in a hug. He takes her by the arm and pulls her along the footpath and into a coffee shop. She finds seats at a table near the window and he comes back with two coffees and her favourite pastry, an almond croissant.

They met when Isobel went to a local nursery to buy some parsley to grow on her windowsill. Nick worked there and Isobel realised he knew everything there was to know about plants. He said she should buy alfalfa seeds because they grow really quickly and they are very good for you. Nick also persuaded her to go to a pub with him the next night and listen to a band. She took her best friend Lucy along in case it didn't work out, but it did and Lucy discreetly disappeared. Isobel told her next day what a great guy Nick was and Lucy smiled her pleasure on behalf of her friend.

Isobel and Nick have seen each other almost every day since that first date, except for the times he went out on mates' nights, and once when he went away on what he described as a stag weekend.

What to do today? There are no decent gigs on, it is too hot for the beach. They sip and talk and nibble and decide on a movie, somewhere cool and relaxing after working all week.

Then they go back to Nick's little flat in Leichhardt. He flings open the window to get a through draft, and the noise of traffic on nearby

Parramatta Road oozes in. He pulls off his shirt, then her dress, peeled over her head like skin from a fruit. Isobel rolls laughing onto the bed, sun-browned arms and legs and white skin which the sun never sees. She looks up at Nick, standing on the end of the bed like a man about to dive into a river, ever the clown. He whoops, crashes onto the bed beside Isobel and rolls her on top of him then smothers her with kisses from her forehead to her belly.

He is the best lover Isobel has ever had. He knows when to be playful and when to be serious.

She wakens next morning to the sound of low-flying planes heading for the airport, and to the weight of Nick's leg lying across her. She looks at the black curls of hairs, like little springs ready to propel him into life when he awakens. He is smiling in his sleep, still with thoughts of their pleasure, she thinks.

Isobel showers, dresses, sits down on the sagging settee and watches Nick. He shows no signs of waking, so she crosses the room and tickles his feet. He stirs, brushes an imagined fly away and turns over. He is oblivious to the low-flying planes, the traffic and the sound of voices in the street below.

Isobel goes to the fridge, takes out a can of beer, goes back to the bedroom and places it on Nick's belly. He kicks like a man who has had an electric shock and bounces upright. 'You bitch.' He grabs her and they wrestle for the beer can as Nick twists it from her hand and tries to force it down the front of her dress.

'You'll rip it!' Isobel protests.

'Take it off then.'

Isobel does. She dances round the room naked then plops onto the settee and reclines in a mock pose of an artist's model waiting to be sketched, but Nick is no artist. His pleasure is in real flesh not flesh on canvas. They make love again, despite Isobel's complaints that the settee is lumpy and prickly.

They breakfast on toasted dry bread, alfalfa shoots and tea because that is all there is in the flat.

'What now?' Isobel asks.

Nick hesitates a moment. 'I'm tied up the rest of the day.'

'You never told me,' Isobel protests.

'Sorry, I forgot.'

'OK then, there's lots I can do without you, I'll meet you back here tonight.'

'Umm, I'm tied up tonight as well, sorry. Tomorrow?'

Isobel quickly gets dressed.

Nick puts his arms around her. 'We'll do something special.'

Isobel wriggles free. 'That's not the point. You didn't think me important enough to tell me.'

'Of course I did.'

'But?' Isobel says.

'It's just something I have to do. Look, I'll cancel.'

Isobel shakes her head. 'No, if you have to do it, you have to do it. I need to catch up on my studies anyway.'

'I'll make it up to you tomorrow. Something special.'

Isobel sweeps up her things. 'Ring me in the morning.'

She spends the rests of the day and evening listening to music in the cool of her room where she shares a house with two others – and wondering why Nick is so secretive.

As promised, he rings her early next morning on his way to the nursery. 'Meet me at my place tonight, pick up some Leb takeaway. I'll give you the money when I get home. You know where the key is.'

He arrives with a bottle of wine, flowers from the nursery and a big grin.

'How was yesterday?' Isobel asks with a smile.

'OK. Did you get much study done?'

'Mmm,' Isobel says between mouthfuls. 'Heaps.'

They make love again.

Over the weeks, the pattern continues. Music in different gigs, takeaway meals and lots of love-making. Isobel finds it hard to concentrate on her studies. Nick gets a promotion at work. He is in charge of the nursery and they eat out big in Chinatown to celebrate then make wonderful love.

Next night, Nick doesn't turn up as arranged at the pub where one of their favourite bands is on. Isobel rings him but his mobile is switched off. She hangs around but he doesn't turn up. There is no one else she knows at the pub, so she goes home early. She keeps ringing into the night but no response from Nick. She feels sick in the stomach. Has he had an accident? She thinks of ringing the police but imagines the conversation. 'Your boyfriend didn't turn up for your date and you want us to check if he's been involved in an accident or an incident?' No, no point in doing that.

As soon as she is awake the following morning, she rings again. No answer. A little later, she rings the nursery.

A male voice tells her, 'Nick's gone to Bali for a couple of weeks with his girlfriend.'

Isobel restrains herself from saying, 'I'm his girlfriend.' Instead she asks, 'Who?'

'Lucy, his latest.'

Isobel hangs up.

She goes to uni but nothing in the lecture or tute registers. But what does register is a burning, roaring anger. Halfway through the afternoon, she walks out. She doesn't go home but to the nursery where Nick works. She buys two huge bags of alfalfa seeds. Then she goes to Nick's flat. The key is where he always leaves it and she lets herself in. A plastic bag from a Thai restaurant is on the draining board with two plates, two spoons and two pairs of chopsticks in the washing-up bowl. She and Nick never ate Thai.

On the rumpled bed is a bra, two sizes bigger than what she wears.

Isobel goes back into the kitchen, flings the dishes from the bowl onto the floor and fills the bowl with water. She goes back into the bedroom and pours the water systematically onto the bed. Then another bowl full. Not until water is dripping through the bed and the base onto the floor does she turn her attention to the sagging, lumpy, prickly settee, and pours bowl upon bowl of water onto it until it looks like something that has survived many a thunderstorm after being dumped in a lane. After that, she pours water on the carpet, squelching backwards and forwards to the kitchen.

Finally, Isobel picks up the alfalfa seeds. She spreads them liberally over the bed, then on the settee, and finally throughout the rest of the room. Backing out the door, she sprinkles a final handful on the floor.

Each morning on the way to uni she goes to the flat and waters the alfalfa. She has a wonderful crop. First the green shoots popped out from the bed, then from the settee, then from the carpet. The D-cup bra is swallowed by pale tongues reaching for the light.

When it becomes a struggle to walk through the knee-high greenery, Isobel forces the door shut behind her one last time. She locks it, and returns the key to its hiding place.

Revenge of the Butterfly

There was once a boy who wanted to catch a butterfly. He had seen butterflies pinned to a board under a glass display case in a museum. He wanted to start his own collection.

A beautiful white cabbage butterfly zigzagged along the street and the boy chased it. He flung his jacket into the air and brought the butterfly down into the gutter. Carefully, he searched among the folds for his prey. As he reached out his hand to take it, the butterfly danced free. It fluttered along the gutter before falling through a grid and into a drain, where it perched like a white leaf on the grimy wall.

The boy took a stick and tried to entice the butterfly to perch on the end but as he leaned over, his glasses slid from his shirt pocket into the drain. No matter how hard he tried, the boy could not retrieve them. Each prod of the stick pushed the glasses further along the drain to where it disappeared into darkness.

Filled with trepidation, he ran home to tell his mother.

She was knotting her headscarf beneath her chin, ready to pick up her bag and step out the door for her shift at the mill. 'Aaahh, you dopey bugger! Do you know how much glasses cost?' she yelled.

He knew. A lot of money.

He led his mother back to the drain where his glasses and the butterfly lay. She knelt in the gutter and peered into the depth. The glasses were within arm's reach.

'Oh, you're such a dope. Always doing something stupid,' she sighed in exasperation, then stood upright.

She bent forward and hooked her fingers through the iron bars and pulled. Nothing happened. She sighed. 'I'm not bloody Samson. Why the devil did you need a butterfly anyway?'

The boy didn't reply to such an obvious question.

His mother tried again. The heavy grate shifted a fraction. She changed her grip and pulled harder. The grate lifted. She tried to swing it clear of the hole but lost control. The grate slipped from her fingers, hit her foot and crashed firmly back into place.

The boy's mother screamed. She dropped to the kerb, slumped forward and buried her face in her thighs. She moaned as she rocked back and forth.

After a while, she sat upright and tentatively touched her shattered foot with the tips of her fingers. She looked up through tear-filled eyes at her son standing open mouthed by her side, 'Do yah never do anything right?'

Eventually, she struggled to her feet, and with her arms draped over her son's shoulders, she hobbled back home.

'I shan't need that for a coupla months.' With her good leg, she kicked aside the bag of sandwiches waiting by the door.

'It wasn't my fault, Mam. The school shouldn't have taken us to the museum,' her son said and burst into tears before turning and fleeing from the house.

When he later sneaked back home, he heard his auntie's voice.

'Maybe there's something wrong wi' him. You should take him to one of those brain people and find out. He does more daft stuff than any kid I know. Remember that time when…'

'Oh, don't go on about it.'

'Maybe you should send him to reform school for a bit. You've got enough on your hands, trying to raise three kids on your own.'

At the sound of the words 'reform school', the boy fled to his room. He jumped into bed, pulled the blankets over his head and sobbed. He would get a paper round and make money to help his mother. Anything but reform school.

The following morning when the sun warmed the air above the gutter, the white cabbage butterfly fluttered from the depth of the drain. It flew into a neighbour's garden, where it laid eggs on the tender young cabbage plants. Caterpillars hatched from the eggs and nibbled the leaves.

The caterpillars in turn became butterflies which fluttered off, to zigzag along the streets of the town in search of gardens.

The Invitation

It was like one of those good news bad news jokes.

Doctor – I've have good news and bad news for you. The good news is that if you take one of these pills every day for the rest of your life, your symptoms will disappear.

Man –That's great! But there's only three pills in the bottle.

Doctor – Yes, well, I was getting to the bad news.

Arthur Cunningham had walked out of the surgery, his mind trying to catch up, that stupid joke going around in his head. His doctor had not told him the joke, but something that was not remotely funny.

Arthur sat on the park bench and sipped a takeaway coffee that he couldn't taste, trying to come to terms with what his GP had said. Everything around him was hyper-real: the squeals of kids playing on nearby swings, the youthfulness and beauty of their mothers, the warmth of the autumn sun on his head, cars murmuring along the distant road, the white clouds that scudded across the blue sky, a crow cawing as it flew overhead; all with purpose and need.

Dr Gupta said the disease was to a large extent unpredictable and different for each individual. Arthur wasn't at the three pills level of the joke.

It was all right for Dr Gupta to be positive. But Arthur knew nothing could be done to prevent a slow decline – or a fast decline. Over the years, he would become a shuffling inarticulate old man, who thought only of the past because the future was unthinkable.

Parkinson's disease. Everyone knew what it was. And he had got it. The name came with a warning, like the small print on a pack of drugs.

It had started with tremors in his hands. Which he ignored for a while and dismissed as just another part of getting old. He had always liked a drink or two, but not enough to give him the DTs, so he knew that grog wasn't the problem. Then he started having trouble walking, not all the time, but enough. So he visited Dr Gupta.

That was eleven months and fifteen days ago. He had not spent that time sitting around feeling sorry himself. A practical man, he had decided long ago what he would do in such an event and had done his research. He accumulated the medication he had been taking as pain relief and would take them all in one hit; that would solve the problem. The big sleep. There was only himself to worry about. Jill had died three years before and they had no kids.

He'd made lots of friends as a journalist but over the years since retirement they were fewer and fewer; some had died, others had retired to the coast where they could walk on the beach, walk in the bush. One of them even tried to walk on water. A sad, cold end.

Others didn't bother to keep in touch any more, with him or anyone else.

None of this changed his plans to have a big farewell party. He went through his list of contacts and emailed or wrote to everyone he had affection for.

He said he had a terminal illness and did not have long to live – without being specific. Everyone would think, cancer.

The party went well, considering the reason for it. Arthur hired a large room in the local town hall and sat at the head of the stairs leading into it to greet his guests. He had a bottle of good red wine and a glass on a table next to it. He felt like a king whose subjects were paying homage. He met everyone with a big smile and an embrace, remembered most of their names, and they were suitably respectful and subdued.

He had spared no expense on the catering: a rock band playing sixties and seventies hits, the best wines, and a wonderful array of food carried around on dainty trays by beautiful, smiling young women and men.

Once all the guests had arrived, Arthur circulated, and chatted. Everyone was too polite to ask him anything personal. They swapped 're-member when stories' with him and each other, and whispered together when he was out of earshot, it's so sad, it's a brave way to confront the end, what a good bloke he is, you wouldn't know to look at him that there was anything wrong.

After a while, a couple of women started dancing. Others joined in. People were laughing and joking like they always do at parties. I'll be forgotten in a week, Arthur thought, and found someone to dance with, Moira, a woman he had worked with when they were in their thirties. Moira had not worn well. He hardly recognised her when she introduced herself at the top of the stairs. When most other journos had moved away from the heavy drinking as they got older and wiser, she looked as though she hadn't. At her retirement farewell in the news-room, she had said to him, 'If I die before you, have a great time at my wake. If you die before me, I'll have a great time at your wake.' He did not remind her of her joke.

He also danced with Joan, who he had been rather fond of many years before. She still worked, although not full time. 'I wouldn't be able to keep up with those young ones,' she admitted.

The party only ended when the man from the council came to lock up the hall. Arthur stood at the top of the stairs and said goodbye to everyone, much as he had greeted them a few hours earlier. There were hugs, firm handshakes and farewell embraces. Some tears fell onto his face.

Joan kissed him on the cheek and said how lovely it had been to meet him again after all the years.

He went home alone in a taxi. He fumbled with the key to the front door. Once he was inside, he sat in his study in the dark. The street light outside cast a pale light over his rows of books and his desk.

He sat there a long time. Eventually, he pulled himself to his feet, went into the kitchen, poured a glass of water, took a plastic bag from the fridge, and slowly climbed the stairs to his bedroom.

Arthur Cunningham sat on the edge of the bed. Outside he could hear a tawny frogmouth calling. It would be sitting all alone on the fence post, thinking no one could see it.

Arthur undressed, hung his clothes in the wardrobe and put on his pyjamas. He sat on the bed again, opened the plastic bag and took out a bundle of small boxes held together with rubber bands. He opened each one, removed the packets and popped the pale yellow Methoblastin capsules out onto the bed. He placed the empty boxes back into the plastic bag. He counted the tablets – accumulated one a week over many months. One by one, he swallowed them, each time sipping from the glass of water.

When all the tablets were consumed, he placed the empty glass on the bedside table and rolled into bed. He pulled the covers up to his chin and lay on his back, looking up at the light reflected on the ceiling. After a while, he felt drowsy and closed his eyes.

*

The sun came up and gradually filled the bedroom with warm light.

Arthur Cunningham lay as he had the night before, on his back, the covers pulled up to his chin.

A fly buzzed around the room, in and out of the shaft of sunlight. Eventually, it landed on Arthur's nose. His nose twitched. His eyes opened slowly. He winced. He sat up, and vomited.

He felt like death. No he didn't. He felt like life, and it was terrible. The pain in his head was so intense he was afraid to move. His guts heaved as they tried to escape his body. Arthur did not know where he was, could not remember what had happened, but he knew he was very, very ill.

Eventually, he managed to sit up. On the floor by the side of the bed was a plastic bag full of small cardboard containers.

What were they doing there?

The answer arrived slowly.

He should be dead. No feelings. No thoughts. Just dead. He wished he was. Anything but the overwhelming nausea in his belly, and a life-time's pain concentrated in this moment.

He closed his eyes again and the bed heaved. He opened them, sat up, and the room spun. Arthur dropped back, grabbed the pillow and hung on until the heaving stopped.

He fumbled on the bedside table for his mobile, knocking over the empty glass, which shattered on the floor. He found the phone and dialled a number he thought he would never have to dial: 000. The phone fell from his hand and dropped into the broken glass on the floor.

The next thing he knew was being slid from the bed onto a stretcher by a couple of burly ambos. With the return in consciousness came the intense pain in his head and the nausea in his belly. One of the ambos picked up the plastic bag from the floor and put it on the stretcher with Arthur as they wheeled him out.

*

'Mr Cunningham.'

Arthur opened his eyes. He was in a bed. By the side of the bed was a figure going in and out of focus. A doctor. She was young. Must have been let out of school early. A nurse was standing a short distance behind.

Arthur's throat felt like it had been sandpapered. His head throbbed. His stomach felt like it had been pumped dry. It had.

The doctor introduced herself. Arthur didn't catch her name.

'How are you feeling Mr Cunningham?' she asked.

Disappointed was the word that came into Arthur's mind. Disappointed and very sick, but he did not say that. 'What happened?' he asked, meaning, 'What went wrong?'

'Would you like to talk about it?' The doctor managed a thin smile.

'Why am I still here?'

'You wouldn't have been but for the fact that the medication was past its use-by date.' The doctor looked down on him and inclined her head to one side.

Arthur could not believe how stupid he had been. All his working life he had checked every fact before filing a story, no matter how urgent. Yet he had been careless when it came to meeting his own deadline.

The doctor told him she had organised someone to talk with him. Arthur was humiliated, because he'd failed and because he was being referred to a shrink. There was nothing wrong with his brain. He had not decided to take his life 'while the balance of his mind was disturbed'. His mind was as balanced as a tightrope walker's. Sometimes he made mistakes like everyone else; on this occasion, big time.

News quickly got around among Arthur's friends that he had had a 'turn'. Some of the people who were at the party visited him when he was released from hospital. They commiserated with him because he'd suffered a turn and had terminal cancer, or so they believed. That was not the way they put it to him, but that is what they said among themselves. Arthur did not explain to anyone why he was still in the land of the living. Nor did he hoard any more medication.

Among the visitors was Joan. Once Arthur was recovered, she took him out to lunch. Then he took her to lunch to thank her. Over the next months, lunch became a regular occurrence, as did going for walks in Hyde Park. She did not mind the fact that he shuffled a bit, nor that what he loved most was talking about the exciting time when they were young journos together. She liked to reminisce too. She also brought him up to date with how things had changed in newsrooms, and what had happened to some of their old colleagues.

A year later, he felt the need to explain to all those who had been invited to his farewell party why he was still here.

He emailed invitations to the Resurrection Party, where he announced that the 'cancer' was in remission and the doctor thought, all things being equal, Arthur could live another ten years. Maybe more.

The party went very well; same venue, same caterers, same good wine, same band. Mostly the same people, except for those who had died, or wandered into nursing homes and not been allowed out.

Arthur didn't want to draw attention to his worsening shuffle by trying to dance. But rock 'n' roll is a powerful force. It gets the heart jumping, it limbers the legs and rolls back the years – almost. Joan drew him to his feet. Arthur remembered what he did on the dance floor as a young man, but, as Mick Jagger said – or was it the Bible? – the spirit is willing, but the flesh is weak.

'You are amazing,' Joan told him.

Who was he to disagree with such insight? So he danced. Joan danced. Everyone danced. No one cared what they looked like. They didn't even think about it.

Moira, who had refused to relinquish old habits, fell over, but that was caused by an excess of wine rather than an excess of years. She was pulled to her feet, and she kept going.

When the Town Hall people arrived to clean up and secure the place for the night, they found the doors locked from the inside. They could hear the thump of the band, the roar of the vocalist, '… we're gonna rock around the clock tonight…' the stamping of feet.

They hammered on the doors but no one was listening.

The Airport

The train from the Central Coast arrived late. Sophie could see her mother hurrying along the platform, anxious, handbag tucked firmly under her elbow. She came through the barrier and smiled.

Sophie hugged her. 'How was the trip, Mum?'

'Usual, except there was this very noisy young couple, swearing and carrying on awful. Drunk or something – in the middle of the morning! The police had to take them off at Woy Woy. They were only in their teens. The couple, that is, not the police. Although they didn't look much older.'

Sophie smiled. 'What's the world coming to, Mum?'

Sophie and her mother transferred to the airport train. Her mother held Sophie's hand as she told her about her week, which was the same as last week, and the week before and the week before that, except that the weather changed: winter, spring, summer, autumn, winter again. Different flowers in the garden; drought-desiccated plants; torrential rain washing them out.

Sophie told her mother about her week, which was a little more exciting but not much. Work.

Sophie bought a coffee for herself and a cup of tea for her mother.

The manager of the food bar greeted them. 'How are you today, Audrey? Hello, Sophie.'

Sophie's mother smiled at him and said, 'Hello, Amal.'

They carried their styrofoam cups to a lounge and sat looking out through the vast glass windows at the taxiing aircraft.

Her mother had her ritual doughnut and licked the sugar from her lips with the tip of her tongue. She dangled her tea bag in the cup full of water before lowering it onto her plate and sipping the weak tea. 'That's nice, dear.'

Sophie unfolded the Sunday paper.

'Aeroplanes are beautiful,' her mother said. 'And so clever. I can never understand how they get up there, and stay.'

'I know. Amazing.'

'And all those people inside.'

Her mother sat looking anxiously through the glass as a rain squall swept across the vast flatness of the airport and battered the windows. 'What a horrible day for travelling. I hope your father's safe. I do worry.' she said.

'I know, Mum.'

'I'm sure he is. He was always a survivor.'

Sophie sipped her coffee and smiled.

'There was that man on the tiny sampan who ate nothing but coconuts for I don't know how long.' She screwed up her eyes as she looked out at the driving rain. 'Imagine it, your father would have been sitting at a meeting in the hotel when it came in from nowhere. He was always a good swimmer. That would help.'

'I'll get you another cup of tea, Mum.'

'Thank you, dear.'

When Sophie returned, her mother was standing close to the window, peering across the almost obscured rain-lashed runway.

'Mum,' Sophie said gently and touched her on the shoulder.

Her mother followed her to their seats. Two young backpackers had curled up on the seats next to theirs and were already asleep.

'It would have been a lot worse than this, wouldn't it? A lot. Hard to imagine really.'

'Much, much worse,' Sophie said.

'Why don't you go for a little walk, dear? Stretch your legs, get something for lunch.'

'Will you be all right by yourself?' Sophie remembered the time when she came back from a 'little walk' and her mother was not there. She was found eventually in a departure lounge for a flight to Jakarta. No one could work out how she had got there.

Sophie wandered around the airport for a while, then stood outside the entrance, sheltered from the rain, watching people as they lined up for the taxis swishing in and out. She wanted to climb into one with a handful of dollars and tell the driver to take her as far as the money would go.

After a while, she returned to her mother, who was sitting looking out the window, the Sunday paper on her lap. The rain had stopped and the outside looked clean and clear. The young backpackers had gone.

'There is always a delay to flights, even when the weather is good. All we can do is wait patiently,' her mother said.

'Like always.'

'Yes. Patience is the word. We must be prepared to wait for what we want. That's what makes you realise how valuable something is, doesn't it?'

Sophie nodded in agreement.

Early in the afternoon, Sophie's mother turned to her and said, 'He's not going to make it today, is he?'

'No, Mum. Not today. Are you ready to go?' She crooked her arm and her mother slipped her hand into the loop.

They walked in slow silence to the airport station.

At the platform for the Central Coast train, Sophie kissed her mother on the cheek and hugged her. 'Same time next week, Mum.'

'Yes, dear, same time. Don't forget.'

'Have I ever forgotten in fifteen years?'

'Not that I remember.' Sophie's mum laughed at her little joke. 'I hope that horrible young couple don't get on the train again.'

'You'll be OK, Mum, don't worry.'

Her mother walked through the barrier and hurried along the platform, handbag wedged under her elbow. She turned before stepping into the carriage, waved, and blew a kiss. Sophie waved back, then turned and headed for the car park and home.

The rest of the day was her own.

The Caravan Park

A big shiny motor home drove slowly into the caravan park. It stopped, then crept forward before stopping again, like a large beast seeking a hiding place for the night.

Eventually, it reversed into a bay. After what seemed a long time, a man in his fifties climbed out of the driver's seat. He stood, one hand on top of the half open door, and looked around. He turned and appeared to speak to someone in the cab before going back to his survey. Eventually, he slammed the cab door shut. He walked to the side of the van, went in and yanked the door closed behind him.

I waited to see who got out of the passenger side. No one did. I couldn't see in through the tinted glass and I didn't want to seem a stickybeak, so I got on with what I was doing, which wasn't much. I was on holiday.

Maybe he'd been speaking to a dog. But not likely. We don't have a dog, but my experience is that they, dogs, are the first to leap out when a vehicle stops.

Before the bloke without a dog arrived, I was getting ready for a barbecue. We have a gas one. Pretty neat. Pulls out from the side of the van. Even when it rains, we can extend an awning and cook there, then sit under it no matter what the weather's like. What more could you want?

It was just about time for a sundowner. Kellie came out of our van with a tray in her hands, right on time. A bottle of white, two glasses, some crackers, olives, cheese. I used to drink beer, but when you're on the road, wine takes up less space.

People in caravan parks are usually really friendly. They want to tell you about where they've been and want to know where you've been and where you're going. They want to compare vans and to brag.

Some of the older ones just wander around Australia. When they can't drive any more, they park in some permanent site near the sea, plant flowers around the van, stay put, and wait. There's worse ways.

The guy who had drawn up across the way from us wasn't old, so he was probably on holiday. But he might have been declared surplus to requirements where he worked, or his coffee shop might have gone bust because of Covid-19. Who knows? That would've explained why he didn't want to talk. He climbed back into the driver's seat and just sat there.

I'd normally have called out and asked him to join us for a drink but I didn't.

I could hear noises from the inside of the van. Whoever else had been in the cab must have moved into the van when I wasn't looking. But the door stayed closed. Eventually, the guy got out of the driver's seat. He nodded in my direction as he walked around to the van and got in, closing the door behind him. It was a hot evening, thirty-five degrees earlier. Why would you want to shut yourself inside? Half the fun in camping is being outside.

'Weird, eh?' I said to Kellie.

She topped up our glasses and bit into a cracker. She said, 'Some people like to keep to themselves.'

Eventually, the smell of cooking drifted from the van. Which reminded Kellie that I was cook for the night and the barbecue was sitting waiting.

'When you're ready, Craig,' she said, and smiled mockingly.

I'm good with sausages and not bad with salads.

No one appeared from the van opposite. Pretty claustrophobic eating inside on a hot night, even in a big van.

Kellie poured another couple of glasses and we started to eat.

I heard shouting and the sound of something being smashed around in the van.

Kellie stopped, with a forked piece of sausage midway between plate and mouth. She looked at me, eyebrow raised.

We both listened. Silence.

We sat as the warm darkness began to wrap around us. A straggle of reluctant kids from the beach wandered past dragging their towels and boogey boards, followed by adults who'd been fishing, rods and buckets dangling from sun-browned arms. I couldn't tell whether the buckets were full of fish, or full of air, because everyone seemed happy. They waved or nodded or said, 'Hello' or 'Goodnight.'

Lights went on in the van opposite but there was silence.

We finished the bottle of wine, cleaned up and went to bed. I read for a while and out of the little window close to my head I could see that the lights next door hadn't been turned off.

They were still on when I was woken in the middle of the night by a noise outside. Probably a goanna, or a fox scavenging for scraps.

When I got up and went out into the morning, the lights opposite were still on, pale in the bright sun. How anyone can sleep with the lights on all night I'll never know.

We had a quick breakfast, packed the sandwiches that we had made the night before and got going.

I put my finger to my lips as we crept by our neighbour's and I strained to catch any sound from inside. All I heard was snoring. Maybe they'd had a big drive yesterday and were sleeping in. They had Victorian number plates.

We set off for a long walk along the cliffs to another bay farther south where we planned to have lunch and get back to the caravan in the early evening.

It was a hot day and the flies drove me mad as we walked. I always forget about flies when we plan a camping holiday. When we reached the beach, a breeze was coming off the sea and that drove the flies away – well, most of them. We got ourselves a possie, me under the shade of a she-oak, Kellie in the sun – I burn, she tans – and watched the surf. It was too rough for me and knee high's the limit for Kellie.

When we had eaten our sandwiches, Kellie lay down and closed her eyes. 'Let me know if anything happens,' she said, and pulled her hat over her eyes.

Nothing did. The most exciting thing was a container ship, far out to sea, sailing on the very edge of the world.

'I still think it's weird,' I said after a while.

Kellie took her hat from her face and sat up. She blinked and looked around, 'What is?'

'That guy last night. The noises in the van. Nobody else coming out. The lights on, all night.'

'Some people can't sleep in the dark. It scares them,' Kellie said.

'What, two adults?'

Kellie stretched out and put her hat back over her face. I know the signs when a conversation's run its course.

I lay on my back as well but it was too hot to sleep. I couldn't stop wondering about our hidden neighbour. I started to think of possible explanations, like:

They were shy.

They were incredibly ugly.

They were being held prisoner.

They just didn't like being on holiday and were sulking.

None fitted.

I drifted off to sleep and was woken by a bad dream in which my neighbour had flung open the door of his caravan and a giant octopus had flowed out. It flashed a huge tentacle at me, encircled my face and tried to cram me into its hot, rough-beaked mouth. I woke screaming and sat up with a jolt. I had rolled off my towel in the shade, and onto the sand and a pile of dry, rough seaweed.

I could see Kellie, a tiny figure walking along the edge of the water in my direction.

We were both tired, hungry and ready for a drink when we got back to the campground. I retrieved a bottle from the mini-fridge and was just about to sit down when our neighbour stepped out of his van. All the lights were turned off now. I raised the bottle in his direction by way of invitation. He paused, then nodded and went back inside. In a few minutes, I heard the clunk of the door closing and he walked across.

He sat down at our little table and put a can of soft drink in front of himself. 'I don't drink. Alcohol I mean,' he said, indicating the two glasses I had set out for him.

'Just you?' Kellie asked.

'Yeah. Just me. My name's Paul.'

We introduced ourselves. Paul tugged the ring pull and his drink fizzed into life.

'It'll save yah a lot of money,' I said, 'not drinking alcohol.'

Paul smiled wanly.

And there was silence.

'To camping,' Kellie said, raising her glass.

'Yeah, camping,' I added.

We all had a sip of our drinks. Then there was more silence. I hate it when that happens.

'Do anything exciting today?' I asked.

'Stayed in camp.' Paul smiled and had another sip.

I wanted to ask whether whoever was in the van had stayed in camp too. I wanted to ask why the person didn't join us – that is, if they were still there. But I decided I wouldn't. Not yet anyway.

I asked him instead whether he was staying long and he said he wasn't sure. He never said 'we', only 'me'. So I guessed that he was alone. Whoever had been thumping around in there yesterday wasn't thumping around today.

Paul obviously wasn't much of a talker.

When I topped up our glasses, he drained his can of soft drink and said it was time he turned in. He stood abruptly, said, 'Goodnight,' then paused.

I thought he was going to say something but he just turned round, and went. We watched him cross the narrow stretch of bitumen road to his van. The lights had been turned on inside.

'Well, what do you think of that?' I asked Kellie.

'You're right, it's a bit weird. Who the devil's in there?'

The rest of the night was pretty well much the same as the night before. The lights were left on, there was banging, muffled, angry voices that went on for ages.

It wasn't the sound of a goanna or a fox that woke me up just before dawn, it was a door slamming. I propped myself up on an elbow and looked out of the little window.

Paul was hurrying to the driver's door of the caravan, struggling to thrust his arms into the flapping sleeves of his jacket. He clambered in, kicked the engine into life and took off in a hurry, thumping over the speed bump a few metres down the road.

*

Next morning when I got up, the van was serenely parked back in its place as though it had been there all night. All the lights were off.

Kellie and me had a long walk along the headlands and were hot, sticky and exhausted by the time we got back in the late afternoon. I was half expecting the van next door to be no longer a van next door, but it was still there. And closed up. But suddenly the door opened, Paul jumped out and headed to the shower block, a towel around his shoulders. A man in a hurry.

I followed about ten minutes later. There was only one shower cubicle occupied; him, I guessed. I had a leisurely warm shower to take away the aches of the walk. Then I had a shave. It felt good.

Paul was still in the shower when I left. How much time do you need to get clean?

I almost called out, 'You okay in there?' But I didn't. It would've been stupid.

Kellie and me were into our second glass of wine when he finally emerged. I beckoned him to come over. A couple of minutes later, he arrived with his can of soft drink and sat down.

'A good day?' I asked.

He snapped on the ring pull and took a drink. He didn't reply for such a long time that I thought he'd forgotten, then he said, 'Yeah. I'm on my honeymoon, ya know.'

Kellie and me were gobsmacked.

'But where's…?' Kellie tried to ask the obvious.

'Your wife?' I finished off the sentence.

'My first wife died three years ago. Those three years, well, two and a half really, were the loneliest of my life. Then I met Amanda. We bumped into each other in a supermarket, literally – trolleys, I mean. We got chatting. One thing led to another. We got married, a week ago.' Our neighbour took a sip of his drink.

We waited.

'She's a bloody alcoholic. Hasn't been sober since we left Shepparton. I didn't have a clue.'

'Six months! How…?' I started to ask

'A one hundred per cent, full blown, falling over, slurring mumbler, card-carrying alcoholic. And I did not know.'

Our neighbour had another sip of his drink. He brandished it in the air like a minor league football trophy, something he was proud of. A soft drink. 'I've never touched alcohol in my life, neither did Sharon. Never.'

I had a sip of my wine, then put the glass down guiltily.

'But…you must, you must, have had some idea. How could you not…?' Kellie asked.

'We didn't move in together, or anything like that, before we married. She's old-fashioned that way. Or I thought that's what it was. So I never saw her, or smelled her, with alcohol. I wondered why she liked peppermints so bloody much. I sold the house, bought that,' he jerked his head in the direction of the caravan. 'We were just gonna drive around the country.' He sighed. 'There's no bloody peppermints now. She's got a grown-up family. They didn't warn me. Glad to get her off their hands, I'll bet.'

'That's awful. What you gonna do?' I asked.

Paul got to his feet. 'I've already done it.' He picked up his soft drink, walked over to his van, stepped inside and quietly close the door.

The van was gone next morning.

Mary's Story

It had been bucketing it down ever since Mary arrived in New Zealand. She was sitting in a bus parked fifty yards from where a brown torrent swept across the road – ten miles from where she was meant to be.

Mary wiped the condensation from the window with the back of her hand and looked out at the green, rain-drenched fields and tree-top clouds. There were only five passengers on the bus.

The Maori driver had assured them that the water level would drop within an hour and they would be on their way. 'Home in time for tea, eh.'

Home. The thought brought a lump to Mary's throat.

The driver was snoring softly now, his head resting on his forearms on the steering wheel. He looked like he did it often.

Mary looked around the bus to take her mind off herself. An elderly woman, still wearing a transparent plastic raincoat, smiled and Mary forced a smile in return before turning to the window again.

*

The town was nothing like she expected. It was smaller, for one thing. The photographs she had looked at in the travel book had been taken in summer and the trees were full of green leaves. Not like now. Anyway, this was the place she had chosen. It was as far away as she could get and she would not be here very long.

As the bus bumped over the bridge, she could see buildings squeezed between low, tree-covered ridges, and below her, the brown, surging river. The main street was deserted, except for a few parked cars and one wet dog sitting under a shop awning.

The bus pulled into the kerb in what looked like the centre of town. The other passengers clambered out and scurried in the direction of the cars. Mary dragged her case from under the seat and struggled down the aisle. She hesitated at the door.

'It's stopped raining,' the driver said.

Mary tried to smile.

'Where d'ya wanta be?'

'The Commercial. It's a hotel.'

'It's that pub on the opposite side of the street, 'bout a hundred yards. You can't see the sign from here but it's the biggest building in town.'

Mary thanked him. She could feel him watching as she lurched along the street, holding her case to her body with both hands.

The Commercial was on a corner, two storeys high, with wooden balconies on one side and a kind of turret on the front. It had seen better days.

As she got close, Mary could read a sign on the main door, Closed Sundays. Tobacco smoke poured from a gap at the top of the door and she could hear the murmur of voices. Mary hesitated, then slowly pushed the door open with the front of the case. A crowd of men was standing along a horseshoe bar. A couple turned in her direction, then, one by one, they all turned. The murmur of voices stopped. Mary carefully closed the door and retreated along the street. She went around the side of the hotel, crunched her way across a car park, opened a door, and entered a hallway with a flight of steps at the end. It smelled of stale cigarette smoke.

'Hello,' she called softly. Mary walked to the foot of the stairs and called louder, 'Hello.'

'Who's that?' a man's voice boomed from above.

'Mary O'Brien. I, I wrote. I, I, I booked a room.'

A tousled grey head appeared over a balcony rail above. 'Ah!' the head said. The man ran down the steps and stopped in front of her. 'You're younger than I expected. Your letter sounded… Oh, it doesn't matter.' He reached out for Mary's case. 'I'll show ya yer room.' He started up the steps, two at a time, then stopped and turned. 'I'm Ron, I run the place – well, me and Bev do.' He started up the steps again. 'You eaten?'

'I'm not hungry, thanks,' Mary said. She had had nothing since breakfast but the thought of food made her feel sick.

Ron unlocked the door into a small room with a large wardrobe, a double bed and a chair. A washbasin was wedged into one corner and a small table with an electric jug and cup and saucer sat along the wall.

'There ya go, all yours. The shared toilet and bathroom's down the hall on the right. Anything ya need, sing out. Bev's me wife. She's keeping the boys happy down in the bar – I mean, serving, down in the bar. Beer. It's always busy Sundays.'

'Thanks, I'll be fine,' Mary said. 'Where, where's the post office?'

'Near where the bus terminated, about a hundred yards, same side.' Ron turned as he closed the door behind him, 'Sure you're not hungry?'

Mary shook her head. She walked to the window and looked out onto an almost empty car park and a dripping tree at the far end. The gloom of late afternoon was merging into an early night.

The room smelled of the same stale cigarette smoke as the hallway. Mary found a single-bar electric radiator in the wardrobe and plugged it in. The feeble red glow made the room seem even colder. She unpacked. She placed her best grey and green wool plaid skirt over a wire hanger and hung it in the wardrobe then slowly transferred the rest of her clothes. The blue sweater was not going to be warm enough.

She hefted Colleen McCullough's book *The Thorn Birds* from the bottom of her bag and laid it on the floor next to the bed. She placed a second book, *The Hitchhiker's Guide to the Galaxy*, by Douglas Adams, in a wardrobe drawer with her underclothes. Inside the cover of the book were a dozen blank, flimsy blue aerogramme letters, handed to her by her mother the night before she left. Mary didn't need the hint; she liked writing letters.

She selected one of the aerogrammes, tugged off her boots and got under the chilly covers on the bed. With *The Hitchhiker's Guide to the Galaxy* as a table, she began to write:

13 June

My Darlingist, lovely Lou,

I'm here. Arrived. Safe. Well. Everything is so strange, you had better believe me. I'm missing you so much already. How can I be lonely when it's only a few days since we were holding each other?

The ship was amazing. I saw dolphins as we sailed out of Sydney Harbour and I wished you'd been there to see them with me. Everything is much better sharing with you.

But the sea was really rough. The top of big waves were blown off by a gale wind. Loads of people were sick. Not me, though. Your Mary might be small, but she's a tough country girl. I bet I could have sailed with Captain Cook, climbing the rigging, high above the deck in the crows nest. 'Land ahoy, captain. Looks like New Zealand.'

The ship was real flash, with all sorts of things to eat on a fancy dinner menu – that's what they called it, dinner, not tea. I've never heard of some of the food. Bet you don't know what sweetbreads are? A clue, they're not made from wheat and they're not sweet. There were snazzy bars to drink at. A bloke bought me a cocktail. Yummy. It made my head spin. On the second night, there was a dance, a sort of farewell, even though most of us hadn't got chance to know each other. Some got to know each other really well, if you know what I mean. But don't worry, I behaved myself.

The hotel where I am staying is sort of OK, but everything is so cold, though the Kiwis don't seem to notice.

Keep writing to me c/o the post office until I'm settled in. The bus got stuck because of floods. That sounds exciting but it wasn't. We just had to sit there watching the water and wait for it to go down.

I've got a frightened feeling inside me and it's horrible. I know that it's because you're not with me and you'd tell me not to be silly. You'll be here soon, and I'll totally forget how scared I am now. I guess you are missing me as much as I am missing you. I wish I was with you, I don't care where.

Every night we can give each other a great big hug before we
go to sleep, even if we are thousands of miles apart.

Here's my hug for tonight. Was it good, even if my hands are
cold?

Your hug was beaut. I want another. And another. And another.
I love you very much.

Your darling Mary.

x x x x x x x x x x

P.S.

This is short because I have to write to Mum and Dad tonight
and let everyone know I am OK.

Kisses and hugs again

x x x x x x x x x

Mary

Mary sealed the aerogramme, placed it on the floor and picked up
another. She lay, propped up in bed, pen in hand, the letter resting on
the book. Except for the drip of rainwater from a broken gutter, there
was silence. Mary put down the pen and turned on her side. She buried
her face in the pillow and cried.

The following morning after Bev's lamb's fry and bacon breakfast
and cheerful 'Yah slept all right?' Mary returned to her room and picked
up the aerogramme she had abandoned the previous night. She
switched on the electric radiator and sat on the edge of the bed, as close
as possible without burning her ankles. She balanced *The Hitchhiker's
Guide to the Galaxy* on her knees and wrote:

14 June

Dear Mum and Dad, Bridgette, Frances, Bernadette, Gerard and Dom,

I have arrived safely, after some delays. I'm staying in a lovely
hotel called the Commercial, but send your letters to the post
office for the time being. There is a great view over the river. The
people who run it, Mr and Mrs McLean, are really nice to me. The
town is small, a bit like Gilgandra, only even smaller. It is colder
than at home and I can see snow shining on big mountains a long
way off, like the Alps in Europe. Everyone is so friendly. I am

going to try and get an interview for a job with the local bank. Mrs McLean said she had heard they were looking for someone with experience, so I am pretty sure I'll get it. Will let you know.

I must finish this now so I can catch the mail and you will get it as soon as possible and know I'm OK.

I miss all of you.

Write and tell me what everyone is up to.

Lots and lots of love.

Mary

She hurried along the main street to the post office, clutching the two letters. The rain had stopped and the air was fresh and cold. White clouds scurried across a blue sky. The river level had dropped but still ran fast and brown.

There was no letter from Lou. Then she reminded herself that for it to have arrived now it would need to have been posted before she left. She smiled at her foolishness. There would be a letter in a few days. She bought a magazine from the newsagents on the main street, went back to her room and lay on the bed with a blanket over her.

Mary could hear occasional guests talking and moving along the corridor. Doors slammed. She couldn't concentrate on the magazine and found a local radio station on her transistor, pop music: 'In the summertime when the weather is hot, In the summertime when the weather is hot.'

The song went round and round in her head. She wished it was summertime. By then Lou would have arrived and everything would be sorted. She fell asleep with the words in her head.

She dreamed, not of warmth and summer, but of a wicker basket floating down a brown flooded river, twisting and turning in the current. The basket went under a bridge but did not come out the other side. In her dream, Mary was leaning over the bridge waiting for it to appear. The dream morphed into a childhood game in which she had played 'sticks' with her friend, each dropping a twig into a creek from a bridge then rushing to the other side to see which came out first, pounding on the rail to urge their stick on.

Mary woke with a start. Someone was knocking on the door.

'Young lady! We're doing dinna if ya wanta come down to eat.' It was the landlady, Bev.

Mary shook herself into wakefulness. 'Thanks, I'll be there in a tick.'

Mary took her seat at a table in the small, chilly dining room that overlooked the main street, the only person there.

Bev was broad in the hips, round in the face and cheerful. Salt and pepper hair sprung like wire from her head. 'What brings ya to our little town?' she asked as she slid a plate of pie, chips and gravy across the table. 'Ya looking for excitement?' She dipped her head to one side and raised an ironic eyebrow.

'I wanted a change,' Mary replied. 'A friend's gonna join me, soon.' Mary wanted to tell her all about Lou, how kind he was, and exciting, and good-looking, but now was not the time. Bev would soon see for herself.

'Nice. You need somebody to keep ya company. Except for the trout fishing, which isn't happening this time a year, the most exciting thing in town's the 1860s goldfields mining museum. Tom Conway runs it. It's open one day a week in winter. He ses it's too expensive to heat. Nobody goes anyway.' She laughed. 'Oh, and there's a dam on the river south of town. That's choice.' She laughed again. 'The place suits Ron and me, though. Do you want me to book a room for your friend, or will you be sharing?'

Bev was fishing, but not for trout. Mary smiled to herself.

'I'm not sure when the person will be here,' she said, avoiding Bev's unasked question. 'Soon, but not sure exactly.'

'No worries. You can let me know. I'll keep a room.' Bev wandered back to the kitchen singing.

Mary began to eat. Every click of cutlery on her plate echoed in the dining room.

*

Each day, she went to the post office and returned empty-handed. Often, she would walk along the side of the rocky river, or onto the bridge, where she would watch the water sweeping past. The river was always in a hurry, wave and surge, then gone in a second, followed by the next. Dashing to the ocean.

Most days, she took the road out of town, walking along the crunching gravel shoulder, past orchards of skeletal fruit trees, leafless branches silhouetted against a cold blue sky. One day, she would walk north, the next day south. When she became tired, she would turn around and walk back to the hotel, where she would curl up in bed with *The Thorn Birds* and read until she fell asleep. She had set herself the task of finishing the outback saga of love and hate before Lou arrived.

Early in July, a letter came from home. The family were relieved that she had a good place to stay and that she expected to have a job soon.

She replied with postcard, a man fishing for trout in the river, shining water and blue sky. She said that she had got the job in the bank and was settling in really well.

Her mother and father had tried to talk her out of her sudden decision to go to New Zealand, said she was too young to be by herself. Couldn't she at least persuade a friend to go with her? Couldn't she wait a few years until Bridget was old enough to go too?

No. She told them she wanted to travel when she was young, before she maybe went to uni. She persuaded them. The whole family packed into the car when they drove her to Sydney to see her off on the ship with streamers and tears. Her dad slipped an envelope of money into her hand before she boarded. It was more than she had saved over the last weeks.

*

The letter she was longing for had still not arrived. She took out a third aerogramme from *The Hitchhiker's Guide* and wrote:

30 June

My Dearest Lou, Lou,
    Still no letter from you. The postman isn't forgetting to empty the box, is he? You must be getting my letters because Mum and

Dad are and they're writing back. I never thought I would have to do something like this. I feel sick at the thought. Once you get here, things will be easier.

There's not much to do, except walk and wait. It's a quiet, quiet little town. Sometimes the only thing I can hear are sheep bleating on the hills. It's probably pretty good in summer, though, when there are tourists. A lot come for the trout fishing, from all over the world, my landlord, Ron, says. I can't imagine anyone from fancy New York or London staying here in this hotel. But Ron and Bev are real nice.

I'm already nearly halfway through *The Thorn Birds*. I thought you'd be here before I finished the first chapter. It's a really exciting book, full of passion and complicated lives. Like ours, I guess. I also listen to music a lot, our songs. My favourite's this one, remember:

> When tears are in your eyes
> I'll dry them all
> I'm on your side
> Oh, when times get rough
> And friends just can't be found
> Like a bridge over troubled water
> I will lay me down

When you get here, I'll read *The Thorn Birds* to you, a few pages every night when we're snuggled up in bed. You can sing to me, in a whisper, of course.

Please, please, make sure you write, and check that the postman is picking up the letters you're sending.

I'm going to mail this now so you receive it soon as possible. The postmistress here is a real sweetie.

Loads of kisses, hugs and love.

Mary

xxxxxxxxxxxxx

*

Mary's daily trip to the post office produced another letter from home, signed by the whole family. Everyone was relieved that she had a job. The annual school dinner and dance had gone well, and her father had been praised by the local MP as the best school principal in the district, 'if not the state', and her mother was happy now that she had started back teaching. All the kids were doing well at school. Bernadette had been picked for the netball team and Dom was playing for the junior rugby league team in the local comp.

But nothing from Lou. Mary anguished about what could possibly have gone wrong. If she phoned him, his mother would answer, because she was always sitting on the phone, waiting for it to ring, a gatekeeper to all the calls that came and went at that house. She'd want to know why is that O'Brien girl ringing you from New Zealand? What is she doing in New Zealand anyway? Talk yourself out of that, Lou.

As she was about to leave the post office, she hesitated, then turned to the postmistress, a tiny woman in her sixties, who smiled at her each time she went in.

'I was wondering, do you have a vacancy?' Mary said.

The postmistress looked up from behind the counter as though Mary had asked to buy a ticket on the next rocket to the moon.

'You know, a position? A job?' Mary added.

'I've worked here since I left school, first as an assistant, then, when Miss Murchison retired, as postmistress. There's only the one position these days.'

'Oh, I see,' Mary turned to go.

'But leave your name, and I can contact you. You're at the Commercial, aren't ya? She slid a card across the counter. 'I'll pin it up on the board.'

Mary filled it in and handed the card back.

'Good luck. I'll keep my eyes and ears open for you as well,' the postmistress said.

Mary walked down one side of the main street and back up the other, her arms wrapped around herself against the cold. She checked out every business that was open, asking if there was a vacancy, including the bank. She met with nothing but head shakes and smiles of sympathy.

On her way back to the hotel, she walked onto the bridge to look at the river. The rain had stopped. The floods had subsided, the water now ran clear and the surface eddies stippled the rocks and gravel below. A trout fanned its gills, its nose pointing upstream, waiting for whatever was to come.

Next morning as Bev served breakfast, she said, 'I hear you're looking for work.'

'How did you know?' Mary asked.

'Dear, I run a pub. If you wanta know what's going on in this town, ask me.'

Mary sighed, 'Yeah. No luck, though.'

'Fancy being a barmaid?'

'I've never been inside a pub. I almost was a few weeks ago.'

'Yeah, heard about that from the boys. They said you looked like a frightened possum.'

'I wasn't frightened, I just didn't…'

'I know, dear. I only take half-a-notice of what they say.'

'You serious? About a barmaid?'

'Of course. It'd be an hour or so lunchtimes, and a few hours in the evening.'

'Yes. Yes. I'll give it a go.'

'Right.' Bev brought her hand down hard on the table. 'Tomorrow. We'll show yah how it's done.'

As she lay in bed that night in her long wait for sleep, she wondered what her mum and dad would think, their eldest daughter working in a pub. What would Dad's staff think at the school? A bit different from a bank. Eventually, she slept, and dreamed of the faces that had turned towards her when she had opened the door to the bar that first day in town. In the dream, the faces started laughing, one by one, until all were looking at her, like the turning clown heads at the annual show when you tried to throw a ping-pong ball into their gaping mouth. The men at the bar were roaring with laughter.

Mary awoke sweating. She flung the blankets clear and swung her legs out of bed, planting her feet on a white rug of moonlight that shone on the cold wooden boards. Her soaked nightgown clung to her body. She eased it free then sat, trying to unravel the frightening dream.

Mary was waiting at the post office when the doors were opened next morning. The postmistress shook her head before Mary had a chance to ask her if there was a letter.

'Maybe tomorrow, eh? We don't have the best service in the world, although I've complained often enough,' the postmistress said.

'Thanks for keeping your eyes and ears open. I've got a barmaid job at the Commercial. Not far to travel to work, eh?' Mary added, trying to arch an eyebrow.

The postmistress beamed. 'That's lovely.'

One problem was solved: Mary would have enough money to pay for the hotel room, without drawing on what she had saved and what her father had given her. Back at the hotel, she dragged a chair from her room to where a sliver of pale sunlight angled across the balcony, and with a warming blanket round her shoulders, she wrote to Lou:

7 July

Dear Lou,
    Still no letter!!!
    But first some good news, I have a job, a barmaid, part-time in the hotel I'm staying at. I'll be a sophisticated lady of the world by the time you get here. It will be a bit of money coming in at least. Working in a bar will not be as hard as chopping trees or dipping sheep, most of the jobs here seem to be in forestry or farming, both men and women. I'm not sure they're the sort of jobs you would like. There might be more work when the weather warms up and tourists come for the fishing.
    But I can't understand why there's no letter from you, or a money order like you promised. I've been here weeks and nothing. I know it takes ages for letters but I'm really worried. Has something gone wrong? I've been expecting you to arrive any day and keep going to meet the bus. They're keeping a room for you at the hotel. I still haven't told Bev anything about my 'friend' who is going to arrive any day. Keep her guessing for a bit of fun.

I haven't applied for any of the papers yet. I want you to be here when I do. We need to do it together. I know there's no rush – well, no, I don't know there's no rush, I don't know anything about it really, but I imagine it will be complicated. I'm not looking forward to doing it.

I've been looking at what cottages there are to let. They're pretty cheap, but I'll wait until we can choose together.

I miss you heaps. See you soon. Can't wait.

All my love, Mary.

xxxxxxxxxxxx

Next morning, she walked to the post office and dropped the letter in the box. Lou's letter and her letter would probably cross paths high above the Tasman Sea. They might wave to each other. Mary smiled at the thought.

A few hours later, Mary presented herself at the public bar of the Commercial. The winter sun streamed through the windows into the long, bare narrow room. It stank of stale beer and cigarette smoke.

Ron was at the far end washing the floor, his long grey hair swung to and fro with each sweep of a steaming mop. 'A minute,' he said.

Mary stood and watched, her stomach knotting at the thought of serving beer to dozens of noisy men.

'All you have to do is smile when you hand them their booze,' Ron told her. After he had stowed the mop and bucket, he showed her how to draw a beer.

'Nah. Not all froth, they won't pay for bubbles,' he said as Mary filled her first glass of beer. 'Taste it.'

Mary did and grimaced. 'That's my best beer, young lady, don't pull a face like that. They all like it, believe me. They're good blokes. A bit boisterous, but that's what happens when ya let off steam. I'll point out the ones that aren't so good. Not a smart thing ta let 'em show you their favourite fruit trees.'

Back in her room, Mary pondered what to wear for her first day as a barmaid, not her best plaid skirt, that's for sure. She opened the wardrobe door, stood side-on in front of the mirror and caressed her belly. She was beginning to show. She half turned and looked at herself from the other side, then front-on. She felt a little kick from whoever was in there, a sort of 'It's me, can't wait to meet you.' A smile began to form on Mary's face. Then it stopped.

Mary chose slacks, a blouse and her blue sweater. Most days, to keep warm, she wore almost everything she had brought. The growing bump could be hidden for some time yet.

She went slowly down the stairs, a knot in her belly rising with every step she took. Working in a pub, what would her mother and father think? What would the rest of the family think?

Men started drifting in about midday. Ron introduced Mary as 'Our little Aussie' and that's what she became, the Little Aussie Girl.

The first beers she drew were all 'froth 'n' bubbles', according to Ron. He finished the pour. The drinkers thanked Mary.

'Not a lot of customers,' she whispered.

'Lunchtime's always quiet, 'cept Sundays, when it's illegal. That adds a bit a flavour to the beer I reckon. Plus the bookie. They'll keep ya on yer toes tonight, though. Not as bad as the six o'clock swill before they gave it the chop. I reckon the six o'clock was OK. I'd finished work by seven. Now it's near midnight an' I sell the same amount of beer.'

Mary knew of the swill in Australia, tired and hungry men crowding into the pubs straight from work, then lurching drunkenly home when they closed at six p.m.

When the last of the lunchtime drinkers had gone, Ron turned to Mary. 'Yer a natural. Ya can already draw a beer as good as me – well, nearly. I reckon you've found your career. Ya could be running your own pub in a coupla years.'

It's not what Mary had in mind but she smiled her thanks.

'Go get some rest ready for tonight,' Ron told her.

She left the bar and headed to the post office. The postmistress shook her head as Mary walked through the door.

'I just came to thank you again. I've done my first shift. Ron told me I'm a natural,' Mary said in an attempt to hide her disappointment.

'Pleased to hear it,' Audrey said enthusiastically. 'The letters will turn up. Sometimes there's a bottleneck with the sorting at Christchurch.'

Mary thanked her again and slowly walked down the main street back to the hotel. She could guess what the postmistress, and Ron and Bev were thinking. They'd be gossiping, discussing all the possible reasons why Mary was alone; waiting for a letter, waiting for someone. She turned on the radiator, then her radio. The local station had the week's top ten: Billy Joe Thomas, 'Raindrops Keep Fallin' on My Head', number one, and had been for weeks. The bouncy optimism cheered her up. She and Lou had sung along.

They'd seen the movie, *Butch Cassidy and the Sundance Kid*, scrummy Paul Newman and Robert Redford, gorgeous Katharine Ross. Lou was better-looking than any Hollywood star.

But where was Lou? Had he confided in someone who had talked him out of coming? His mother? His dad? Lou would never do that any more than she would.

Maybe he was just going to arrive and surprise her. Lou liked surprises.

Mary slept and woke late afternoon with a sour taste in her mouth and nausea. Rain was tapping the windows and the hills were shrouded in cloud. She lay on her back and rested one hand on her stomach, then the other. She gently massaged the soft white skin.

Bev was already serving early customers when Mary took tentative steps into the bar.

'Ya eaten?'

Mary shook her head. She was hungry but did not want to eat. 'I'm too nervous.'

'Nothing to be nervous about. Ron said you did a great job lunchtime. You're gonna need all the energy you can get before the night's out.'

Some of the customers who had been there at lunchtime asked her, 'How's our little Aussie goin'?'

'She's going great,' Mary replied.

She did as Ron had instructed. She smiled as she drew their beers, not all bubbles and froth. Coins were left on the bar for her. She was too busy thinking of beer and thirsty men to be able to worry about anything else and before she realised it Ron was calling time and urging the men to drink up and go.

As Mary was leaving, he handed her a beer glass full of coins. 'Yer tips. I don't get that much in a year. Told ya, yer a natural, the best barmaid in town, but don't tell Bev I said so.'

Mary clutched the glass to her belly and walked up the stairs. Half a dozen blokes had asked her if she had a boyfriend. Three of the younger ones had asked for a date. Where would you go on a date? She had smiled in response. In her room, a large inverted plate and a glass of milk were on the table by the bed. Mary lifted the plate. Beneath it was a huge meat sandwich.

The single-bar radiator had been replaced with a fan heater.

*

Each day was much the same as the day before; Mary went for a walk in the morning. As she 'happened' to find herself passing the post office, she would step in to say hello to the postmistress. Mary never asked, 'Is there…? She knew that the moment a letter arrived she would be told. There was nothing to do but wait. Each day, despite Bev nagging her to eat, she became thinner. She worried that as the bump in her belly got bigger, she would look like a worm that had swallowed a golf ball and no amount of clothing would hide it. But that's what was going to happen and once Lou arrived it wouldn't matter and everyone would know anyway, if they didn't already.

She wrote more letters to Lou and worried: was he coming?

Was he sick?

Had there been a serious accident?

Had Lou been killed?

The thoughts tormented her day and night.

Mary took out another aerograms and wrote:

31 July

Dearest Lou,

What am I to do? Nothing from you all these weeks, surely if something really serious had happened and you can't write you would have got someone else to do it, or even phoned the hotel. I'm at my wits' ends. What am I to think?

I really need to talk with you about the baby. I've been waiting until you come. It's not something we can sort out when we are half a world apart, or in letters, but there's not even letters. I can't go on like this, waiting and waiting – for nothing?

Please PHONE ME.

All my love,

Mary

xxxxxxxxxxx

Mary shrugged into her coat, buttoning it up as she ran down the steps, along the hallway and out into the car park. She hurried along the main street to the post office and thrust the letter into the mail box.

Before she could turn round, someone called out, 'Mary! Mary!'

Audrey, the postmistress, was standing by the door, brandishing a letter, smiling.

Mary grabbed it. Lou's writing. She gasped a thanks to Audrey, turned and ran. Not until she had slammed the door of her room behind her and was alone did she open the letter.

21 July

Dear Mary,

I'm really sorry to have taken so long writing. It's what you thought might have happened. I pranged the Holden, ran out of road and hit a tree. My left leg's broken, the radiator's history, so is the front mudguard, and the bonnet looks like an elephant sat on it. It's not a write-off but it's going to cost a bomb to fix. I'm out of hospital now but still on crutches. That means I can't join you, I wouldn't be much use anyway.

I hope you're settling in. Glad you got the pub job. You'll be able to work for a bit before you get too big. Have you got the adoption papers yet? It will only need you to sign them, I think, not me as well. You can do it and when the baby is taken care of and you come back here, everything will be OK.

We made the right decision about adoption. A kid would have been too much and we're too young to get married and have all that responsibility.

I'm enclosing a money order. It's not much but it will help when you stop work.

I hope you're getting used to the cold. It's cold here too.

I miss you.

Love

    Lou.

9 Aug

Dear Lou,

I'm really sorry to hear about your horrible accident. Sounds terrifying and painful, but you're still alive, thank God, that's the main thing. I couldn't bear to even let myself think about the worst that could happen. And thanks for the money order. What a relief to hear from you.

But why didn't you write and let me know at the beginning you were in such a mess? Just a few words would have stopped me worrying.

Got to keep this short. I'll have to run or I'll miss the post.

Write back to me straight away and let me know when you're coming, crutches and all. Better still, ring me at the hotel, best before lunchtime, or after.

    Love,

       Mary

       xxxxxxx

15 Aug

Dear Lou,

Still nothing from you, only one letter in almost three months!

The lack of words says everything. I've tried to avoid facing the truth but I can't any longer.

You could have come to me after a few weeks, even with your leg in plaster. I didn't need you to do anything for me, I needed you to be with me.

I didn't want to face all this without you, but now it seems I have to. I've made new friends, who I am sure have guessed what has happened even if they don't say anything. Unlike you, they will support me, I'm sure.

Being by myself with so much time on my hands has made me think a lot. I think of my baby, curled up nice and warm inside me. I also think of what will happen to her when she has been handed over to her adoptive parents. It's not like giving someone a pet dog. Have you thought about the new parents? How well they will look after her? Or not look after her. Whether they'll be rich, or not? Have you worried about any of these things? I have, night and day, for weeks.

No matter how good the adopting parents might be, they could not look after my baby like me.

I've decided I won't be coming back to Australia without her. I will come back, one day. With her, or him. I am NOT going to give my baby up, I never wanted to. I said that in the beginning but you talked me out of it because you don't want to be a father. You don't want responsibility.

I'm letting you off the hook. You can swim off by yourself. I am not abandoning my child. And don't worry, I'll not be asking you for money.

No one will know who the father is. I might even claim immaculate conception, like my namesake. If she could get away with it, why not me? My child will never know what a weak and cowardly man you are, because she will never know who you are. You are a nothing. I am disgusted with myself for letting you so close to me, ashamed for loving you.

You can't face up to difficulties now and you won't be able to in the future. You're not much of a man. In fact, you're not much of a boy. If you live to be old, you still won't be a man.

Don't ever dare come near us. Don't ever dare claim you are the father of my child.

You have no idea how much I hate you.

I feel dreadful for the shame I'll bring on Mum and Dad.

They'll have to put up with kids sniggering behind their hands during school assembly, and the nudging and staring during Mass, good, God-fearing people crossing the street to avoid them.

I'll have to face the same thing too when I get back. I can, unlike you.

This is my last letter.

Don't reply.

Mary.

Mary strode through the sleeping town towards the post office, her final letter to Lou in her hand. She dropped it into the mail box.

Clutching Lou's money order and letter, she walked back through town, turned onto the bridge and stopped halfway across. Below, the surging water gleamed pewter in the moonlight.

Mary shivered.

She looked around to see if anyone was watching, then held Lou's letter and the money order above her head and shredded them. The pieces fluttered down to the water.

A trout darted to the surface. It swallowed Lou's words and money.

Going Home

Karen knew what the two words meant. Nevertheless, she kept Googling them, just to make sure. There could be different meanings for the same words; you chose which you agreed with. Simple as that.

Anyway, word meanings change over time. Gay, for one. It no longer means happy, although most gay people are probably happy these days. Another example, nice, used to mean stupid; awful used to mean terror.

She put her laptop to one side on the bed and tried to stretch her legs beneath the confines of the sheets. Through the wide, open doors, she could see the balcony and, beyond that, suburbs and the city, ethereal in the smoke from distant bushfires. She felt lucky to have such a view, but she knew it was the result of thirty years of high premium health insurance payments rather than luck.

She thought back to words again, and doctors. Doctors are not infallible. They'd probably got the diagnosis wrong. They are mere humans like everyone else, although some of them thought otherwise.

Karen had become used to the tubes inserted in her nose, and being propped up in bed day and night so her lungs could function.

There was no pain now. And if there was no pain, there was no reason to stay in hospital, even if the view was better than at home, nor to move to another hospital where, she had been assured, they were better equipped to deal with someone in her condition.

She was sure she'd be going home any time. Tomorrow even. The end of the week at the latest.

Margaret was a good sister. She was looking after Titch and the house. Margaret said she was taking care of the garden, but Margaret didn't have green fingers. Her idea of a garden was a couple of shrubs that looked like toilet brushes, stuck into tubs on each side of the door. And square white pavers of identical size that you could hose down once a week.

Karen's plants needed watering, weeds needed pulling. She worried about what would be alive by the time she got home. Titch, on the other hand, was easy to look after; he just needed walking, feeding and cuddling. In a few days, maybe a week, Karen knew she would be strong enough to look after the garden, Titch and herself. She closed her eyes. Thinking was tiring.

When she awoke, the sun was disappearing behind the tall buildings on the horizon and the sky was crimson. Someone was sitting in a chair by the side of the bed looking out of the window. She was wearing a long white dress. Titch was curled up on her lap, his nose on his paws, eyes closed.

Margaret turned and smiled. 'Welcome to the land of the living,' she said, and immediately wished she hadn't.

'You should have woken me,' Karen said.

'You looked so peaceful. You kept smiling and muttering to some-one. Who was it? A handsome man?'

Karen snorted. 'I don't remember my dreams, even good ones. How long you been here?'

'A while.'

'You must have been bored.'

'You need rest.'

Karen snorted again. 'That's all I get, rest. And advice. But I don't care what they say, I'm coming home. Isn't that good news?'

Margaret smiled. 'What have the doctors said?'

'That everything's fine.'

'What exactly have they said?'

'That they want to get me out of here, move me to another hospital. But I'm not going. What would they know? I know how I feel. They don't. Is Titch behaving?'

Margaret picked up Titch and deposited him on the bed close to Karen.

'You missing your mummy?' Karen kissed Titch on the nose.

Titch licked her face, then curled up on the bed and closed his eyes.

Margaret smiled. 'He sleeps on your bed every night. Won't come in with me.'

'He's a big sook, aren't you, Titch? You'll have me home with you at the weekend, won't you?' Karen gently tugged his ear.

'I'm watering the garden.' Margaret pulled a tissue from the box on the side of the bed. 'Honest. It's hard to keep up, though. With this heat, it dries out so fast no matter how much you give it. And there's water restrictions.'

'I'm not worried about that.'

'Good. Do you want me to brush your hair?'

'There's not much left to brush. Is it a mess?'

It looked like it had been chewed by rats but Margaret didn't say that. She took a brush and mirror from her bag, sat on the edge of the bed and started to gently stroke the fuzz.

'I hate people coming to see me like this, tubes stuck up my nose, my bloated face, my hands scaly. Nearly bald. I'm a freak!'

'It's a hospital, not a beauty parlour. They come to see you because they love you. They don't care what you look like.'

'Is that a compliment? I care. When I get home I'm gonna dye my hair. What colour do you reckon?'

'Natural. Not pink or blue like old women.'

'I was thinking platinum blonde. And short. Short's very fashionable.'

'You're halfway there.'

Karen tried to smile. 'I'll go on a diet too, get rid of all this revolting flab. Look at it.' She stuck out her neck to expose the rolls of flesh around her throat. 'You won't know me. And, right from the start, no alcohol. Except for the first night. That'll be a champagne occasion. You can get a case in for me, there's money in my purse. After that, strictly clean living. A walk every morning and evening with Titch, lotsa vegies and fruit. I'll show 'em.'

She slid the laptop towards Margaret. 'Google palliative care.'

'Again?'

'Just do it, please.'

Margaret lifted the lid off the laptop and typed.

'Read what it says,' Karen said in a firm voice.

'All of it?'

'Yes.'

'Are you losing your memory or something?'

'My brain's fine.'

Margaret read, 'Palliative care: medical caregiving approach aimed at optimising quality of life and mitigating suffering among people with serious, complex illness. Within the published literature, many definitions of palliative care exist. Most notably, the World Health Organisation describes palliative care as "an approach that improves the quality of life of patients and their families facing the problems associated with life-threatening illness".'

'If they don't know, no one does,' Karen said. 'That's what this hospital stuff is doing, improving life,' Karen said.

Margaret gently closed the laptop, and smiled at her younger sister.

'When you come tomorrow, bring my red dress, and the black boots. I'm gonna leave here in style,' Karen instructed. She smiled.

The Man Who Was

Your first reaction will be to think, I made this up; or, less politely, I'm a liar. I didn't, and I'm not. Everything I'm going to tell you is the truth. I remember every moment, I was that kind of child, even though I was only three when it started. I'll explain.

My mother was running through the park close to the harbour with me in my stroller. I could hear the slap of her feet and the sound of her gasping for breath behind me. She thought that sort of thing was good for her. It was exciting for me, the wind in my face, my hair blowing around, my eyelids peeled back because she was running so fast. I nearly bounced out of my stroller. My mother was like me, she did all things full on. She overtook everyone, men and women.

Then she fell.

Because she was moving at great speed, she lunged forward. The stroller with me in it shot out of her hands and accelerated towards the end of the jetty and the harbour.

Unknown to me, she was lying flat on her face, with red-raw knees and a bloody nose. I was too busy yelling with excitement to notice. The pace of the stroller got faster. I yelled louder. I didn't know that I was travelling solo until the pram hit a timber beam that lay along the edge of the jetty to stop stupid grown-ups from walking into the sea.

The stroller, with me strapped in, catapulted into the air. I shot through space and down into the cold water. I began to sink. I opened my mouth to scream. It was a stupid thing to do. I closed it immediately. Too late. By then, I had swallowed a lot of salt water, a couple of fish and a baby cormorant. I was in deep and going down fast.

My descent suddenly stopped. That was the moment I met my father, although I didn't know that's who he was.

Something was propelling me upwards. Through the bubbles I could see a hand clutching my stroller and dragging me and it behind. Another hand was pulling frantically through the water. Two feet were kicking back and forth close to my head.

We reached air and sunlight. In front of me was a swimmer, goggled, yellow-capped and wetsuited. I screee-eamed. After a struggle, he freed me from my stroller, then he rolled onto his back and, clutching me to his chest, swam to the jetty, where my mother had climbed down a ladder and was clinging to it with one hand while reaching out to us with the other.

She grabbed me by the back of my jacket, pulled herself up the ladder and hoiked me onto the jetty like the catch of the day.

I regurgitated a bellyful of harbour water, the two fish and the surprised baby cormorant in an explosion of vomiting.

'Oh no! What you going to do next?' mMy mother moaned as she held her hands over her mouth.

She looked down on the previous contents of my stomach, then flipped fish and baby cormorant back into the water with a Nike-clad foot. The fish sank and the cormorant flapped away over the harbour on soggy wings to tell its story.

Moments later, my rescuer swung himself onto dry land and dragged off his goggles and cap and stared at my mother. 'Martha!'

'John!'

'Where did he come from?' he gasped.

'You're a man. You should know,' my mother snapped.

'I meant just now, how…?'

He stopped asking questions and looked hard at me. I could guess why, my hair was red and curly – just like his.

'Is he…?'

My mother didn't let him finish. 'Of course he is, who else?'

'How would I know?'

'Thanks.' She used the word like a slap across the face with a fish.

'You never told me.'

'You never asked me.'

'I didn't see you again.'

'You didn't look.' Mum glared at him. 'It was a wild party, wasn't it? Or have you forgotten?'

'I haven't. What's his name?' The man who was my father nodded in my direction.

'Noah.'

'As in…'

'Yes.'

The conversation ended then because I started to bawl even louder. I was freezing 'n' sneezing.

My mother pulled me into her sweaty bosom and, hugging me to her so hard I could hardly breath, she started to run for home. Or she tried to, but her fall had hurt more than her pride and all she could do was hobble.

'I'll dive back in and see if I can find the stroller,' the man who was my father shouted.

Mum must have given him one of her don't-be-stupid looks, which I was going to become familiar with in the future, because I didn't hear her speak, yet the man who was my father didn't dive back into the harbour.

Mum slung me across her shoulder and limped in the direction of home. I could see the receding figure of the man who was my father in his glistening black wetsuit and yellow cap. He was running, not towards me, his new-found son, but in the opposite direction, away from me. He dived off the wharf into the harbour and began to swim frantically. Imagine the effect that had on me at such an impressionable age – for the first time, I met the man who was my father, and he fled. The last I saw of him was his distant figure splashing towards a watery horizon. I was traumatised.

In my hand were his goggles. I must have grabbed them in my terror.

Mum didn't notice until we got home. She snatched them from me and flung them into a corner.

I protested by throwing the only thing I could throw, a tantrum, which by the age of three I was pretty good at. I couldn't swim yet but I felt I would need those goggles one day.

Mum told me to shut up. She wasn't usually like that. She was upset, not just because of the fall, but because meeting the man who was my father obviously revived a bad memory. It had been a one-night stand – I didn't know what that meant at the time.

From that moment, I did not stop searching for the man who was my father. I slipped out of preschool by standing on an empty milk crate, reaching up and opening the gate. Because everyone was dealing with the Covid-353 infection, almost the entire workforce of the country was furloughed. We looked after ourselves at preschool. It was good preparation for later life.

When I wore my father's goggles, I found I could swim with ease. I checked out the area where I first met him because that might have been his favourite swimming spot. I stripped down to my undies, hid my clothes in a garbage bin then swam around and around. He had to be somewhere, unless he had just kept swimming away when he realised he was my father. I had to find him to find out what sort of a person he was, what genes I had.

You've got to remember it was a time of great uncertainty. Apart from having to cope with the 353 variants of Covid, adults were trying to come to terms with something people claimed was caused by the disease: age-flexibility. At that stage, they hadn't yet worked out that some children, like me, were born with the brain of an adult, but without the life experiences of an adult. It complicated things for them.

I wandered each day, searching everywhere people were allowed to swim. I was back before my mother picked me up. No one noticed I was gone. I got rid of adults who soft-talked me with the intention of taking me by the arm and leading me to someone in authority. Swear words were the best attack. First they were in shock. Then in disbelief. Then I was gone.

I went to ocean swim races and walked along the beach checking out the line-ups of eager contestants waiting to dash into the ocean, hoping one of them would be my dad.

Officials, seeing me wearing goggles and walking back and forth, asked, 'What age group are you looking for, son?'

My mother obviously did not want to see my father again. She kept on running, but never ever in the place where she fell on her face and I was flung into the sea, and I met him.

My father did not want to see either my mother or me because he never again swam in the place we met.

Didn't he believe my mum about the party?

Didn't he care about me?

Didn't he care about her?

Could I bring the three of us together?

It was up to me.

I checked out my mum's laptop when she was asleep – she was always exhausted. Maybe she ran too much.

There were lots of videos on running, on parenting and on Covid mutations (loads of those) but nothing in her emails or social media pages about the man who was my father.

I asked her if she'd help me find him.

'Definitely not,' she said.

When I told her that every boy needs a mother and a father, she laughed. When I said, every boy needs two parents, one on each side to keep him upright, she laughed again, then scooped me up, put me in the stroller – just to make me feel small – then went for a run. She never tripped and fell again.

When I was five years old, I left home, not because I didn't love my mum, or because she didn't love me. I just had to find out what my father was like. Mum didn't run after me despite how much she loved running. With the help of make-up and a few other devices, I managed to look like a small man. People stared, and nudged and sniggered or obviously tried not to, but other than that no one bothered me.

After running away, I contacted my mother and she agreed to send me enough money each month to keep me afloat – as long as I didn't ask her to help find my father.

I went to a police station to see if they could help. They picked me up and sat me on a chair and started asking stupid questions about me being lost, and helping me 'find mummy and find daddy'. I ask you! No wonder bad people are running around all over the world when police can't tell the difference between a small adult and a large child.

My early toddler searches for my father in the water had left me with not only a love of swimming but with a great capacity for it. I joined a well known surf lifesaving club. Not as a nipper, but as a full-grown adult because I was such a brilliant swimmer. In my first summer, I saved seven people from drowning – wearing my father's goggles. Something good had finally come from our accidental meeting.

One scorching Sunday at the height of summer, I was on patrol when the call went out that someone was in trouble. I rushed down the beach, launched my board into the water and powered through towering breaks. A man was thrashing around and screaming. I yelled to him that he was going to be OK. I dragged him onto the board, and paddled back towards shore. A breaking wave swept him off when we were a hundred metres out from the beach. I grabbed him, pulled him back on again and paddled in.

The man was covered in bluebottle jellyfish stings; their long sticky tentacles were pumping poison into his body. He was in anaphylactic shock and moaning like he was going to die. A paramedic placed an oxygen mask over his mouth and told him to slowly exhale and inhale.

The man's eyes were wild. 'I'm dying. I'm dying,' he gasped.

'Is he?' I yelled.

'What?'

'Dying?'

'Naa. But he thinks he is. He can't breath sometimes. It's not much fun, I can tell ya.'

I went with the patient and the paramedic in the ambulance to the hospital.

The patient kept gasping, 'I'm dying. I'm dying.'

I didn't believe him any more.

Nurses sat him in a plastic chair under a warm shower to wash the poison off his skin. I waited nearby to see what happened next. When he was breathing like a normal person, the nurse took off his cap and oxygen mask. I'd have recognised the red curly hair anywhere, just like mine – it was my dad.

We spent the remainder of the day talking about swimming.

Dad said he planned to be the first person to swim around Australia and was setting off next morning.

I wished him well, shook his hand and said goodbye as he climbed into an ambulance to be driven home.

I never saw him again.

I never saw my goggles again either. A pity; they were real good goggles.

I didn't tell my mother that I'd finally found the man who was my father.

My swimming was nowhere near as good after I'd rescued him. I eventually left the surf club. To be honest, they asked me to. I took up running instead and, though I say so myself, I'm pretty good. The club coach is great; she's my mum.

I'm planning to run around Australia.

Footnote: If you are pregnant parents reading this, don't worry that your child may turn out like me. My condition is extremely rare. You are unlikely to have to put up with this type of behaviour.